*A
Harlequin
Romance*

OTHER
Harlequin Romances
by JOYCE DINGWELL

Many of these titles are available at your local bookseller, or through the Harlequin Reader Service.

For a free catalogue listing all available Harlequin Romances, send your name and address to:

HARLEQUIN READER SERVICE,
M.P.O. Box 707, Niagara Falls, N.Y. 14302
Canadian address: Stratford, Ontario, Canada.

or use order coupon at back of book.

FLAMINGO
FLYING SOUTH

by

JOYCE DINGWELL

HARLEQUIN BOOKS TORONTO
WINNIPEG

Original hard cover edition published in 1974
by Mills & Boon Limited.

© Joyce Dingwell 1974

SBN 373-01867-3

Harlequin edition published April 1975

Printed in Canada

CHAPTER ONE

ALL the way back from St. Paul's Pillar, which had been Georgia's final Cyprus offering to her sister-in-law since after tea they left the island for Greece again, Leone had been preoccupied. Even Aphrodite's Rock, rising Dover Cliff-white out of a pastel blue sea, had not left her rapturous as before, but, smiling sympathetically, Georgia had not resented Leone's abstraction. Frankly, she had not expected that mother hen ... tagged fondly, of course ... to have lasted this long. She was supremely unsurprised now that the family was calling Leone in a silent but not-to-be-resisted voice.

'I wonder how John is coping,' Leone fidgeted, missing the damson bloom on the distant Troodos Range, the sight of a donkey carrying as well as his load of aromatic herbs four well tucked in, dark-eyed children. 'I wonder if Adrian is running round in his bathers all day – he will, you know, if you don't watch him. I wonder if—'

'If Bronwen's nose is sunburned,' came in Georgia, 'if Trevor's toe has been stubbed on the rocks. Darling, do stop worrying! John will be seeing to all that.'

'Who' ... a little chokily from Leone, for Leone was a sentimentalist ... 'will be seeing to John?'

'You. From tonight on.'

... But who will I be seeing to? Georgia had thought.

She had not anticipated thinking in such a strain, since for some time now she had schooled herself not to, and, or so she had considered, had graduated with honours. But now there was an odd restlessness in her instead of that imposed acceptance, a less-than-composure in place of her carefully nurtured serenity. Perhaps John had been right and she shouldn't have come back to Cyprus. Yet still, she knew,

5

though it might be just that she had no one pulling her away from it as Leone had, she didn't want to leave.

Her brother had been astounded when she had told him she intended kidnapping his wife for a week on the island, not astounded at the offer, for he could see, as Georgia could see, that Leone needed a break from the children, but at Georgia's choice.

'Cyprus?' he had echoed.

Then: 'Georgia, do you think you should?'

'Yes. Why not, John? All that is finished, the page turned, nothing left.'

'It was glorious weather,' recalled her brother .... he had been there as well, it was really because of him that Georgia had gone there ... 'something like the ambrosial weather this year.' He had paused. 'Georgia, it could turn out a reminder of another summer. You could be hurt.'

'No,' she had smiled.

'Places bring back memories.'

'Of themselves as well as people in them. I love the island. More important, for Leone, I know it. How much better to take her to somewhere I'm familiar with.'

'I see your point, but—'

'John dear, Leone obviously needs a break. This Aegean holiday you're giving your family, and' ... appreciatively ... 'me as well, is simply wonderful, but so long as there's one of the three offspring around, that girl of yours just won't relax. A week away from them would be fabulous for her.'

'Agreed, and accepted with thanks. But why not Rhodes? Crete? Even across to Tel Aviv for some night life?'

'Because I know Cyprus, and I can make it much more interesting.'

'And – reminding?'

'You did say you agreed,' John's sister had ignored blandly, 'now all we need is Leone's approval.'

Leone, at that stage, if still enjoying the Aegean bay that

6

John had booked nonetheless finding a certain harassment in keeping three lively youngsters intact while living only fifty enticing feet from the sea, had eagerly approved. Georgia had no doubts that since then she had enjoyed herself completely, but the children called now, and husband John. She was ready for the Aegean beach resort again, the watching of her wild ones as they romped in the bay, the pouring of sun filter, the bandaging of knees, the running-after with canvas hats. Family, in short. Of which Georgia had none.

They were nearing Limassol now, the port city with its attractive gardens, its wide sea front hemmed with outdoor restaurants, its gay shops, but this time it was Georgia instead of Leone who gazed out and did not see. Georgia was looking back on another summer instead.

John, in his trade advisory post, had not taken his family with him from Australia for his few months on Cyprus, Munich was his next, and much longer, assignment, so Leone and children would wait till then. But as Georgia was visiting England anyway that year, why not take time off to see her big brother and to bring a breath of home?

She had brought it, she hoped, and certainly John had assured her she had.

... Just as Justin, an English rep this time, had assured her that she had brought him a breath of something just as sweet. A breath of spring, he had smiled.

Justin Reynolds was not with the same firm as John, but their terms of Cyprus duration were similar.

'Mostly, for our particular calling,' John had explained to his sister, 'Cyprus comprises only a passing-through, or at the most only a brief seasonal stop.' He had said it *significantly*, had Georgia only had the sense, as she had it now, to realize what he had been trying to tell her. He had been warning her not to take things seriously ... not to take Justin seriously ... but she had been eighteen, the summer had been idyllic. And she had fallen in love.

Justin never had encouraged it, she had to be fair about

that, but on the other hand he had met her halfway, and with an eager smile in his bright blue eyes, an electric touch in his fingers. They had gone everywhere together, done everything together, that remembered summer on the island, from speedboat racing at turquoise-watered Famagusta to antiquity searching at Alasia, the Bronze Age city. But finally it had been across at Bellapais, on the island's northern side, that Georgia had known that the celebrated Tree of Idleness, under which they had sat for coffee, for her had been instead the Tree of the Moment of Truth.

She had been chinking the ice in the accompanying glass of water to the small cup of dark sweet brew when she had remarked: 'A nice custom, Justin. We'll adopt it in our home later.'

He hadn't said anything, but it was even more clear than if he had. The silence almost had poised there above them Georgia had had the ridiculous idea that if she had reached up she could have taken that silence in her hands and read its label. The label would be: 'Oh, Gigi' ... Justin had called her that ... 'I never intended this.'

She had sat on, growing progressively more uncomfortable, feeling her cheeks grow redder than the pepper berries under which their table was placed. From Bellapais on a clear day you could look to Turkey, but Georgia had averted her head to look out only as far as the Gothic cloisters of the Abbey. Her eyes were filled with hurt tears.

Justin had been just as kind to her on the way home, but when she had said to him, 'Good-bye, Justin' instead of 'Good night', he had known what she meant. He had put his hand briefly on her shoulder, then left. She hadn't seen him again. John had reported that he had gone on to Athens ... then on to ...

'Mostly, for our particular calling, Cyprus comprises only a passing-through, or at the most only a brief seasonal stop.'

'Yes, John,' Georgia had confirmed on that second occasion that her brother had told her, 'you said so before.'

But this time she heard.

She had lasted out John's term with John, there were only a few weeks left, then returned with him to Sydney. Then her brother had received the Munich post, gathered up his family and left again.

Georgia had settled back in her job, and it was not for any broken heart that she had not married, she had simply met no one she wanted, and so it was when Leone had written out: 'As a career girl rolling in money, why can't you visit us while we're here?' that she had gone overseas again. John's holidays had coincided, and he had brought the family down to Kassandra Beach, south of Thessaloniki, and from there Georgia and Leone had sneaked off to Cyprus, and this evening would sneak back.

They were now turning into the street where Georgia had selected their hotel for their Cypriot stop. She had chosen Limassol as the most central city and the Curium as opposed to any sea-front inn after Leone's mere fifty feet to the bay at Kassandra.

Once in their hotel room, Leone got busy with her bags, and to conceal a little smile at her eagerness, Georgia went and stood at the window to gaze out. The Limassol Gardens were almost opposite, their trees spilling dark green pools of shade. There was a small zoo and aviary, and into the summer quiet came the drowsy stir of animals and the cool chatter of birds.

It had been a lovely day, as lovely a summer day as that remembered summer. Irresistibly, Georgia began thinking of more island scenes to which Justin had treated her ... small dreaming villages clinging precariously to hillsides with tiers of whitewashed cottages touching their cobbled streets ... patchworks of barley and wheat seen from a hill-top whose gentle slopes were silver from olive groves or blurred pink from the first of the almond blossom ... castles that seemed to grow out of rock and to touch the sky.

'I don't want to leave.' The words escaped her.

'Did you say something, Georgia?' Leone looked up from a case.

'Yes,' smiled Georgia. 'Would Bronwen like one of those figurines we saw down in St. Andrew Street yesterday?'

Leone made a helpless gesture. 'You've already been far too generous.'

'I didn't ask you that, darling.'

'I know. Then – yes. But you're not going now?'

'It had better be now. It's fifty miles to Nicosia and the airport, and we'll have to start as soon as we finish tea.'

'Then don't get lost there,' appealed Leone, who had nearly got lost herself in some of the narrow offshoot lanes and among the dense crowds.

'I'm an old Cypriot, remember,' returned Georgia, and stepping back from the window she took up her shady hat, for St. Andrew Street was a few summer-hot blocks away.

'Shall I pack for you?' Leone called as Georgia went out of the door.

'No ... that is ... I mean ...' As she got into the small lift to descend to the lobby, Georgia wondered why she felt so foolishly uncertain of herself.

For most certainly she was returning to Thessaloniki with Leone, later returning with the family to Munich, later leaving for Australia again. Yet still she felt – unsure.

No need to hand her key in this time to the clerk at the desk, Leone was still upstairs in their room, but, from habit, Georgia half paused there, and the receptionist, glancing up, said in the perfect English you encountered everywhere here in Cyprus: 'Now, why did I not think of you, Miss Paul?'

'I beg your pardon?'

'Our gentleman guest with the two children ... of course you would be precisely what he would require.'

'Bright, intelligent and attractive?' laughed Georgia, joining in the mystery.

The clerk's dark eyes indicated unmistakably that this could be so, but aloud he indicated factually: 'Australian.'

'Australian?'

'On your passport.'

'But—' Georgia began.

'You are, aren't you?' he insisted.

'Why, yes, I am, but then so is Mrs. Paul.'

'But Mrs. Paul is not Miss Paul, and this gentleman—'

'With the children, two of them,' Georgia prompted mischievously.

'Certainly with the children, for they are why you would be required, would only accept an unattached person.'

It's becoming curiouser and curiouser, decided Georgia, but she did not say so aloud; after all, it was asking a little too much to expect the English-speaking Greek clerk to know *Alice in Wonderland* as well.

She went out into a leafy avenue, down by the Gardens to Limassol's wide waterfront, past the giant figure advertising the Wine Festival ... remembering the summer when Justin had taken her there ... then by the stone sea wall to the teeming shopping area. St. Andrew Street. Most exciting street, she had thought once ... Justin beside her ... in the world.

It was still exciting. The street was so narrow, cars literally had to inch through; there were no sidewalks, so it was rendered more canyon-like still from streams of pedestrians.

But the shops were fascinating. Sweetmeat shops, cake and pastry shops, shops selling delicate embroidery and exquisite lace, shops selling cheap tin trays. Dresses made. Suits made. Boots made. Sheepskin rugs. Leather-ware.

At length she came to the more exclusive shop where yesterday she and Leone had spent an enchanted hour over lovely silver filigree brooches, intricate gold chains, flawless lapis lazuli fobs and gleaming turquoise pendants. The figurine that had appealed to Leone as a gift for Bronwen was in the furthest display, and Georgia edged past many chattering groups of shoppers, for the store was popular with tourists, to mull again over the small china people, so faithfully moulded and finely presented, in their brightly-lit corner shelf.

The shepherdess with the lamb in her arms had appealed to Leone, but the child with the ball, considered Georgia thoughtfully, might appeal more to her young daughter. Then there was the boy playing the pipes; a small, dimply moulded but quite exquisite donkey, very typical, she decided, of Cyprus; a china bell-wether you could well imagine taking his rightful lead, his little neck bell ready to chime, in front of the flock. A small exquisite Jesus in tender blue porcelain.

'. . . So if you could help me . . .'

The voice cut clearly into Georgia's enjoyable mulling, but it had not, she saw at once, been directed at her.

It had come from a man, a tall man, rather too tall and too broad-shouldered for a place of fine things like this. He must still have been addressing the group of women he had been speaking with previously, for his words came at the end of what he had had to say.

'. . . So if you could help me . . .' he appealed to them.

The group, all in holiday spirit, were obviously eager to help him. In the desultory way you listen, or at least words reach you, Georgia gathered that two gifts were required for two children, boys, but if such a thing was possible in a store like this, a more tough, or a more manly, gift was called for.

'Because these two, I'm afraid, have been outrageously hothoused, and I want them to begin to face up.'

The tourists were an all-American contingent, deduced Georgia from their voices, which was a little surprising, since Cyprus was not so much patronized by the States. But Georgia learned, as she still considered the shepherdess, that they had crossed from Jerusalem for a taste of the Mediterranean, and since they all came from Wyoming, the inquirer must have known he would get a good answer from a Westerner, where men were tall and tough and very male. Or so they assured him, and laughed.

As they argued amicably between themselves on the pros and cons of plaited crops, wallets, leather camels, other male-slanted gifts, Georgia came back to the delicate figurines, feeling rather incensed. Although she had not chosen anything china for Adrian or Trevor ... heaven forbid! ... she still liked to think they could appreciate it without being tagged 'outrageously hothoused'. She had no time for parents who only concentrated on the tough side, or so they strove for, of boys. Still fingering the shepherdess, she heard one of the American ladies ask the man the boys' ages.

'Six and seven.' – Georgia tried to work out the man's accent, but failed. But she did not fail to stiffen. Six and seven, yet expected to be tough. Poor babies!

There was one of those sudden lulls that busy places occasionally stage. In it, and to her horror, not so much for the expense, for it was not such a dear piece, as for her extreme embarrassment, in her resentful stiffness Georgia suddenly dropped the shepherdess. She was bending over the shattered pieces when the man ... the one with the tough sons-to-be, or so he hoped ... came forward, and, edging her aside, brushed the fragments into a handkerchief where they could do her no injury.

'Thank you.' Georgia said it sparsely, but at once the brown head shot up. The man looked sharply at her.

'Not American?'

'No.'

He waited very obviously for more than that, but Georgia said no more. Pushing past him, she signalled the attendant across.

'Unfortunately I've—'

'It is quite all right, madam,' the attendant assured her.

'But I've broken it.'

'It is all right.'

'I'm sure this is not your usual procedure,' protested Georgia.

'If Madam will select her figurine—'

'I had selected that one, but then I broke it. If you'll take a cheque—'

'I have told Madam it is all right.'

'It's also wise to make sure you have your cheques before you offer one,' the voice she had not been able to identify suggested dryly. The man, upright again now, handed back the travellers' cheques she must have dropped when she had mishandled the figurine – with it her passport, her hotel receipt.

'Thank you.' It was inadequate, but she could think of nothing more. Annoyed at her clumsiness, angry at the fact that in that short time he could have noted her name, nationality, everything else about her, she stopped arguing with the attendant, whom she could see she would not influence, anyway, so she pushed her way past the crowds again, then once more emerged to St. Andrew Street.

She had not gone far, for in St. Andrew you could not hurry even if you wished to, when a taxi, inching along as all the cars were forced to inch, pulled up.

'It's not a long walk,' called a voice she remembered from her encounter in the store, 'but driving gets you there quicker, I find.' The man who had picked up her shattered shepherdess remains opened his taxi door.

'I'm quite all right, thank you,' she said coolly. 'I wouldn't care for you to go out of your way.'

'It's my way, too – the Curium. Could you get in at once, the traffic appears to be banking up.'

It certainly was, Georgia saw . . . what else could be expected in this narrow canyon? To save further congestion she accepted the lift, if unwillingly, and the taxi moved off again.

'Thank you for picking up my ruins,' she offered stiffly as they edged towards a much wider thoroughfare, but almost as congested again as the canyon, since it was shared now by buses, vans, trucks, bicycles, handcarts and laden donkeys.

'Thank you for being an Australian,' he said calmly back.

She looked at him in complete surprise, and he nodded coolly.

'We can't waste time,' he intimated next, 'on preamble. Already I've learned from your sister-in-law that you're booked to leave after tea for Nicosia Airport, thence to Thessaloniki. So what I have to say must be at once ... or at least in the hotel.'

'I don't understand you.'

'How could you ... yet? But until you do, let me assure you I was very pleased when you shattered that gew-gaw, and had to speak up, otherwise I could have gone round for an hour searching for a Strine.'

'I beg your pardon?' stiffly.

'Beg away,' he shrugged. 'But please to change your outraged tone of voice, for I'm one, too.'

'Australian?' She refused to use that 'Strine' that he had used.

'Yes.' At her look of doubt, he added, 'Only years abroad have filed off my rough edges.'

'Meaning—?' she flashed indignantly.

'Oh, no,' he assured her easily, 'your tone is all right, though there's a little unevenness there. But not to worry, I find it quite livable-with.'

She looked out at the busy street in anger. 'I don't understand any of this,' she repeated, but it was not the Cyprus traffic she meant but the situation in which she found herself. This man who apparently had been in search of her. His mention of Leone. His knowledge of their imminent departure. His succinct: 'We can't waste time.'

15

'Then briefly, very briefly, our hotel clerk contacted me ... I saw your sister at once ... on her directions I came down here to see you. But where, among all those women, was I to find you?'

'So you thought up two children to be duly toughened?' Georgia said coldly. 'Then you asked around?'

'Yes,' he confirmed calmly.

'Quite a story,' she awarded.

'Except that it's a true one. They do exist.'

'The boys?'

'Yes.'

'Ages six and seven?'

'Yes.'

'And a need for toughening?'

'Again yes. And that's what I want to talk to you about.'

'I see.' She absorbed this for a moment. 'And do I look that type then? That toughening-up type?'

'No. And that sets me back a little, I'll admit. But beggars can't be choosers.'

'Really—'

'Yes, really ... but quiet a while, please, for here we are now. We'll go straight to my suite if you don't mind. We can talk better there. No, it's perfectly all right, there's a private sitting-room, and besides your sister-in-law, the clerk knows where you will be.'

'This is going too far!' she protested.

'We've gone nowhere at all yet, but I hope we will. At least hear me out, if nothing else.' He had paid off the taxi, impelled her into the white and gold inn, and was now leading her to the lift. 'I know you're due at Nickers in several hours,' he said, 'but what I need can be finalized in a third of that.'

'It is?'

'I said in my suite, Miss Paul, but you may as well mull things over until we get there. Only don't for pity's sake

16

drop what I propose as quickly as you dropped this figurine.'
He reached in his pocket and took out a shepherdess, a new, intact shepherdess.

'You—' she gasped.

'Yes, I bought it for you.'

'You also probably signalled the attendant not to charge me for the breakage.'

'Just before I picked up the cheques, passport and hotel receipt to assure me that I had the correct person,' he nodded back.

'For what?'

'You rather surprise me. Up till now you've been very astute. The answer is the boys, of course. The hothoused fellows of six and seven due to be toughened up.' A short laugh. 'You should have seen your scandalized face at that!'

'You weren't looking.'

'I was.'

'With your back turned?'

'I have eyes there, too. When you're in my employ, it might be well to remember that.'

'When I'm in—' she began indignantly, but he stopped her by preceding her out of the lift to lead the way down the hotel corridor.

At the end of the passage he opened the door to a large suite and bowed her in.

Two children ... boys ... were playing rather desultorily on the floor.

'Bysshe ... Segovia,' the man said distastefully, making no pretence, Georgia gathered, that he would prefer a Bill or Jim. Then, not altering his voice, which was distasteful to Georgia, since in John's family the children were always considered as equals, equal rights, equal sensitivity, equal privileges and privacy, he tossed: 'Look them over for a few moments before you accept my offer, Miss Paul.'

Accept *his* offer! Georgia could have answered immediately that nothing could be more remote. However, she did look at the boys.

Experienced now in John's and Leone's trio, two of them fairly age-comparative young males, or so she judged, she decided that this pair were rather smallish for six and seven. Also pale. But paleness, as opposed to pallor, had little to do with health, she knew by now; possibly they had forfeited any colour they normally possessed by being cooped up in a hotel.

'Many hotels,' the Australian drawled knowledgeably, knowledgeable of the trend of Georgia's thoughts.

'Bysshe, of course, coincided with his mother's poetic phase,' he went on. 'Being an individualist, or so she liked to think, she didn't want just Percy or Shelley.' His tone was astringent.

'And Segovia?'

'Her Spanish guitar period. But please not to be discouraged. The pair will answer to Bish and Seg. Or' . . . a threatening look at the unattending pair . . . 'answer to me.'

'Mr.—' began Georgia indignantly, then she stopped. She did not know his name.

'Plain Smith,' he smiled, 'a bit of a comedown after Bysshe and Segovia,' but Georgia found she could not smile back. She did not like this discussion of the children in front of them like this.

'Don't worry.' Again he drawled it knowledgeably. 'They're not even listening. Oh, no, they're not slow, just introverted, psychosomatic, complex, maladjusted, self-centred little pains in the neck. Also,' he added, 'spoiled rotten and bored to tears.'

'At six and seven,' Georgia disbelieved . . . but unwillingly she secretly agreed they looked an unrewarding, lacklustre couple. However, to make a child, two parents are needed, and though she was no feminist, Georgia did not believe that this man should get away with everything.

It appeared, though, that all he was getting away with now were the two children.

'They're my responsibility until I'm ready to take them to Australia for a period. Hence' . . . he had taken out a pipe and was lighting it, and for the first time Seg . . . or was it Bish? . . . looked up with interest . . . '*you*, Miss Paul.' He noticed the boy's curiosity over the pipe, and tossed, 'Probably only ever experienced Turkish cigarettes before, and I think I *mean* experienced.'

'You wouldn't know.'

'But I still wouldn't be surprised or put it past the blasé little sophisticates.' A pause. 'Well?'

'Well what?'

'What I've just proposed.' A show of irritation. 'Oh, you mean salary, duration, the rest.'

'I mean – anything. You've told me nothing at all. No' . . . as he opened his mouth . . . '*not* in front of the boys.'

'You flatter them. But if you insist—'

'I do.'

'Then hi!' He glared down at the pair. 'Hi, kids, hi, Bish, hi, Seg, *out*!'

They looked up at him a moment, then did as he said.

'See,' said Mr. Smith after they had gone, 'not even any fight back.'

'Now you're being too unreasonable. It appears to me you want it every way.'

'Why not? My parents had it in me.' His eyes narrowed from the smoke wave from his pipe were directed banteringly on her. Georgia knew he was deliberately baiting her.

Presently, maddeningly unaware, or anyhow, pretending to be, of her fuming dislike of him, he resumed.

'The children have been dumped on me. Yes, literally dumped. I can't send them over to Australia unaccompanied; I also have nowhere at this juncture there to send them. I can't go myself for some months yet, I have essential work here.'

'There are schools—'

'European. For born Australians, I consider they've already been in Europe too long.'

'An Australian school, then?'

'In time. But they must be prepared first.'

'Then you *are* concerned about them,' she commented.

He gave her a glowering look, but she knew she had gained a point there, that point that for all his brusqueness this pair was not as completely unimportant to him as he would have liked to convey. At least he had a few shreds still left of decent fatherhood . . . or was it in his case just personal pride?

'I don't wish to take them to Australia, even for that short period, in the way they are now,' he said shortly.

. . She understood what he meant, and smiled patronizingly.

'How long have you been out of Australia?' she inquired.

He gave her a quick hard look, and she said, 'For some time, I think. Australia is as sophisticated, blasé, false' . . . she paused, then went on triumphantly . . . 'introverted, psychosomatic, complex, maladjusted and self-centred as the rest.'

'You left out,' he pointed with his finger, 'spoiled rotten and bored to tears. But I see what you mean. You think that I consider Australia as the sole last frontier. I don't. I believe every word you just said, but I also think that as Australians . . . which they are . . . they should be prepared for it, which they are not.'

'Mr. Smith, all Australian boys don't go round looking like prize-fighters or buck-jumpers, in fact most don't.'

'Then answer me this: Do many go round looking like Bish and Seg?'

'Well . . .'

'You see?' Again he pointed the finger. 'I don't ask the

impossible. But I do want a bit of colour on their faces, a bit of muscle on their arms, a bit of interest in them.'

'I suppose I could help with the colour and the interest,' she admitted.

'Then that would earn you what I propose to pay.' He told her; and she wished he hadn't, because it was a *very* attractive sum, and she didn't want, and anyway wouldn't take, *his* job.

'I,' he concluded, 'can see to the muscle myself.'

'I'm sure,' Georgia said next, 'that if you look around you'll find someone much more suitable than I.'

'I'm quite sure of that, too,' he said deflatingly. 'By choice I would never select your type, not, anyway, for this purpose.' He nodded to the door through which the boys had left.

'Nor any purpose?' she suggested, incensed.

He shrugged.

'However,' he went on, 'I can't waste any more time than I've wasted already, so it has to be you.'

'It has not!' she exclaimed crossly.

'Your sister has told me you're not at all anxious to leave Cyprus.'

'Leone wouldn't know.'

'You underestimate her,' he contradicted, 'she gathered more than you thought.'

'Then if I'm not anxious, I'm certainly not un-anxious.'

He ignored that. 'You haven't a home, as she has, children, as she has, a husband—'

'Usually the husband comes before the children.'

Again he ignored her. 'So there's no reason in the world for you to refuse.'

'Leone told you a lot of things in a short time,' Georgia said after a long resentful pause.

'It had to be short. It has to be short now. The tea gong goes in exactly' . . . he checked on his watch . . . 'ten minutes. After that you leave Limassol almost immediately for Nicosia Airport, thence Greece. Or'... he waited a deliberate moment ... 'you don't leave.'

'I leave, Mr. Smith,' she assured him.

'At that salary?'

'It is attractive, I'll admit, but I still leave.'

'Liking this place? Still experiencing a pull from this place?'

'There's no pull,' she insisted.

He smiled, but said nothing, and it was worse than if he had.

'Anyway,' Georgia burst out when he still did not speak, 'I could overcome that, overcome any – any pull, as you put it.'

'Overcome filling a void, which I hear you now have in your life?'

'Really, Leone—'

'Overcome a call to help these children?' He brought that out last.

She hated him for that, hated him for his uncanny knowledge, even not knowing her, that those two lacklustre, rather unlovely children could be an armour chink.

'Bish and Seg,' Mr. Smith said factually, 'require you, Miss Paul. If you can oblige them, you'll oblige me.'

'I—'

'It would be your privilege to choose any type of background, either villa, apartment, hotel suite ... houseboat, if you like; also any location, any situation, seaside, mountainside, city, hamlet, plains. Again, you will be provided your own car.'

'You make it sound just too fabulous. Apart from browning them up, interesting them, talking Australian—'

'Strine was my word,' he grinned.

'What else?' she ignored.

'A mother's love?' he said sarcastically.

'A father's love is just as necessary,' she retorted as caustically.

22

'All right, we'll skip that angle. Just prepare them for something more than they've been having; it doesn't essentially have to be the Wild West. Get them so that they won't arrive Down Under looking like indoor plants. I don't want he-men, I want normal, less-than-white, scratched, faintly grubby, smelly little boys.'

'As you were?'

'You get the idea. Your answer?'

'No.' She meant that, she could never work for a man like this.

The tea gong was going. He let its resonance sink in for quite a few moments.

'So,' he accepted, spreading large capable hands, 'another day wasted.' He got up and shrugged defeat. 'You'd better hasten, Miss Paul, the car departs promptly at sixteen hours.'

She had hesitated, she could not have said why, but now his words prompted her up, and she moved smartly to the door.

About to pass through it, she became aware of something at the other door, the door through which this man's sons had been impelled, and, compelled herself for some reason, she turned round.

They both stood there, Bish and Seg, two undersized, undesirable young fry, not saying anything, not even looking anything particularly, but suddenly she knew it was just no good.

She knew he knew so, too, knew it before he said breezily and hatefully: 'So! So we stop after all, do we?'

'I am neither regal nor plural,' she said haughtily.

'You'll need to be to do anything with *them*.'

'Mr. Smith, if I do do anything, and I'm not saying yet that I will, it has to be *not* under these circumstances.'

'I told you that you can choose a villa.'

'Not under the circumstances of talking in front of children like this.'

23

'I told you that they—'

'I know what you told me, but these are my conditions.'

'Then I agree. Beggars can't be choosers. Will you write your name there, Miss Paul?'

Georgia did, thinking what a fool she was to agree to such an uncomplimentary offer, to consider two difficult children (though she had never known yet a child you could not get round in some way) . . . to consider one difficult man (she found she had nothing to add to that).

She stood looking at him. He looked back at her.

The gong kept resounding, and presently Georgia said a little unbelievingly, unbelieving that she was actually doing this thing, actually agreeing to this farce:

'I'll go and tell Leone not to send down my bag.'

24

CHAPTER TWO

GEORGIA'S first contact with the boys was taking them with her when she accompanied Leone into Nicosia Airport to wave her sister-in-law off to join her family again.

When she asked Mr. Smith's permission for this, he said, 'Yes . . . though if you're thinking it will amuse them—'

'Of course it will amuse them, all boys love airports.'

'You'll find these two have seen so many all they'll register will be an even greater degree of boredom.' He added, 'If such is possible.'

Georgia did not argue; you should not with an employer; but she had never found a boy yet not fascinated with the rush and bustle of an air terminal, the sounds of engines warming up, the sight of taxiing aircraft, then, when you ran to the spectator platform, the thrilling sight of a plane taking off, or landing, or climbing, or descending, or simply waiting in readiness on the field.

As soon as she had taken tea with Leone, fitting as much talk in as the time for a quick cup would allow, she went up to Bish and Seg to superintend the changing of their play shorts for something more suitable for a farewell. But one glance told her that with them it was unnecessary. They were both immaculate. She even had no need to instruct them to wash their hands.

'We're going into Nicosia Airport,' she announced.

'It's a small one,' demeaned Bish.

'But an international,' added Georgia. 'Do you know what that means?'

'Of course. We always come down at internationals,' withered Seg.

'My sister-in-law is leaving in a Trident 2,' Georgia said hopefully.

25

Bish said, unimpressed: 'Oh?'

Seg said: 'I knew that.'

'Would you like to see it leave?'

This time they made the same reply.

'Not much.'

In the big car, Georgia put the two of them in front with the driver. All small boys are intrigued with cars, especially cars like the expensive model that had waited outside the Curium to take them into the capital.

All boys ... save two. They never even glanced at the instrument panel.

Her sister-in-law, very aware of the more-than-interest her own pair always evinced, conversely the need to keep their inquisitive fingers in check, darted Georgia an uneasy look. 'I was so thrilled when Mr. Smith told me about this post, Georgia. Now I'm not so sure.'

Georgia, unsure herself, said determinedly: 'It's early yet.'

At the airport, the boys just sat on the seats, legs poked out in front of them because they were adult-size seats and they were small people.

'Would you care for some lemonade?' asked Georgia.

'If you want.'

'I'd sooner *you* want,' Georgia appealed.

'Then I'd like a cigar,' said Seg.

'He smokes chocolate ones,' tossed Bish.

Relieved, Georgia doubted aloud if the sweet section here would stock chocolate cigars.

'It doesn't matter,' said Seg indifferently, and though she supposed it was better than a scene because he must have a chocolate cigar, Georgia did feel a little like Mr. Smith must have felt when he had called 'Out' and they had got up and gone.

At last she gave up, and left them still sitting there with their legs poked out, staring, it seemed, at nothing, and went and sat with Leone.

'After all,' Leone was reiterating, 'you only have to step on to a plane.'

'Darling?'

'To get away.' Leone looked apprehensively at Bish and Seg.

'I'll do something with them; I've only to find what they're interested in.'

'Do you think they're interested in anything?' Leone still looked concerned. 'My only consolation is Mr. Smith,' she brightened. 'He really is *some* man. I mean the way he got things done. And, Georgia, he's promised before he leaves for Australia with the boys to send you up to Munich to us.'

'If I last out that long?'

'I agree. That pair—'

'It wasn't the pair I was thinking of,' Georgia said.

When Leone was called to the plane, Georgia insisted that the boys come with her to the spectator platform. They did so as though they were being marched into class, and once at the rail stood looking at anything, Georgia thought, save the departing Trident.

'Well, that's that,' she declared over-brightly as the plane became a distant speck. 'Shall we have the driver pull up on the way back at a sweet shop for cigars?'

'I don't care for them,' said Bish.

'I don't want one any more,' said Seg.

Georgia pointed out a few antiquities on the way back; however, she did not blame the boys for their lack of interest – anything past their own memory, she knew from Adrian and Trevor, was not worth bothering about.

'Also,' said Bish, 'we've been to Athens and Rome and everywhere.'

'Everywhere?'

'Yes.'

'England?' she asked.

'That a town, too.'

27

'It's not, Bish, and here's something very thrilling.' They had reached Amathus, outside Limassol, and Georgia told the story of Richard the Lionheart. The Crusades should stir any boy, she thought triumphantly.

It didn't.

When they reached the Curium, she took the boys to the suite, intending to leave them there either with their father, or a hotel attendant, while she retired to her own upstairs room that she had shared with Leone. She had not yet worked out her hours of employment with Mr. Smith, or learned what was expected of her, but she did not think the ordinary nursemaid chores of washing, feeding, putting to bed would be included. Not that she minded them – indeed, she would have preferred them; there was more to be gained from a child in the un-griming of knees . . . though certainly these two would never need un-griming . . . or the tucking in of blankets, then in any prepared occupation.

Before she could open the suite door to nod the boys in, it opened for her.

'Back,' said Mr. Smith.

'Safely accounted for,' reported Georgia. She paused a moment, then turned to leave.

'Where are you going?' he asked.

She turned back. 'Why – nowhere, if I'm required.'

'You're not required, but if it was to your room you were bound—'

'It was.'

'Then I've arranged for your accommodation on this floor. Oh, no, not in this suite, but across the passage.' He put a finger on her elbow, and it was a cool, impersonal but authoritative finger, and impelled her out again, then to the room opposite. Except that it was not just one room; once more he had taken a suite. Not so large as his own – he had his sons to cater for – but dressing-room, small sitting-room and balcony.

'It's very nice,' she admitted.

'It will do till we move,' he shrugged.

'To where?'

'That,' he said, taking out his pipe, 'is where you will be needed.'

'How do you mean, Mr. Smith?'

He had crossed to the bell pull as soon as he had ushered her in, and now the porter knocked and entered.

'I thought perhaps a pre-dinner drink,' Mr. Smith said to Georgia, 'there are a few things I wish to discuss.'

'What about the children? Can they be left?'

'I've arranged for them to be fed by one of the hotel staff at a time I believe is termed nursery tea.'

That 'to be fed', thought Georgia, sounded rather like the feeding of small animals in a zoo. It irritated her, but she inclined her head.

'Then I'm not expected to attend to that?' she asked.

'You're expected only to give them a foretaste of what they'll get later.'

'How could I know that?' . . .

He gave a gesture of impatience, and nothing more was said until the Cyprus claret he must have asked for was brought in.

'How did the boys behave?' he inquired perfunctorily when the waiter had left.

'Perfectly.'

'You didn't add "of course".'

'Of course,' she conceded with a ghost of a sigh.

Ghost-like, or not, he heard it, and warned, 'It might not always be so.'

The humour of that reached her, the humour of wanting two children to behave *im*perfectly, and she half-laughed . . . until she found he was laughing, too. It was the first time they had met like this, and she found herself rather enjoying it.

'Well, we'll see,' he said. 'But meanwhile I want you to choose where you want the boys, all of us, to live in Cyprus.

I told you this before. I don't know the island, you do, so our future address for the time until I'm ready to leave for Australia will be in your hands.'

'But you must have a preference,' she insisted.

'I told you, I barely know the island.'

'But your work—'

'I'm fortunate that my work needs no especial location.'

'You're with no representation?'

'No. Nor any firm. I need nothing that will be obtainable more easily from a city than a village, or vice versa. You see, I'm a writer.' He was looking at her keenly.

She nodded. 'But wouldn't somewhere quiet and secluded be much more suitable?'

'I can work just as well in a noisy hotel.'

'Then you're not temperamental?'

'I write about current factual world affairs, not romantic fiction.'

'But reference libraries—'

'I carry my own with me ... or should I say on me?' He touched his head.

'You're very fortunate,' Georgia commented.

'No – assiduous.'

'I should have remembered. Your parents got everything in you.'

'Your parents received a child with a good memory.' He topped up her glass.

Cyprus wines were heady. Over the full rich red she looked at him and asked, 'Should I know your writing?'

'Not if you're strictly a fiction reader.'

'I like all reading.'

'I use Smith,' he said sparsely.

'And select current topics?' she pondered.

'The only Smith I've read of that type,' she said presently, 'is the famous Agrippa Smith.' – On a sudden thought she looked up at him. 'Not—'

A pause, then: 'Yes, Miss Paul.'

'But – not Agrippa?'

He did not answer, and now Georgia did not just half-laugh, she went into a happy peal of laughter. 'And you decried Bysshe and Segovia,' she challenged.

'You could say,' he said distastefully, 'it runs in the entire family. I instructed my publisher to use the name Bill . . . William is my second name . . . but he grabbed on the other. Need I add that my parents were students, that at my debut their interest was early Rome.'

'No, you needn't add that.'

'Anyway, that's the explanation. I prefer Bill.'

'And get?'

'Grip. Which, at least, is not effeminate.'

'Which, of course, matters.'

He ignored that. 'Should you need to call me by name and find yourself unable to reconcile that need with Bill, Grip will do.'

'I shall call you Mr. Smith,' she decided.

'Very well, Miss Paul. Now, about the residence to be. You need not restrict yourself – I'm a fairly lucrative writer.'

'Best-seller?'

'I keep up a steady income which I consider is better. You may prefer the city, the hills, the beach – it doesn't matter, it's not a large island, and there's always transport.'

As she sat silent, wondering where, he came in a little abruptly with:

'Already, I should say, you've selected a place from your last visit, for you were here, your sister informed me, the entire summer some years ago.' He paused. 'No doubt now you would be searching for a reminder of that summer.'

Reminder of summer. John had said that, he had warned her about it, he had not wanted her to come to Cyprus because of it. Reminder of summer – that lovely, lovely summer when she had known Justin.

She became conscious that Agrippa Smith was smiling

blandly across at her. Putting down her glass so abruptly that she spilled a little, she said, 'I'll think about it, let you know.'

'Do,' he invited, then he got up.

'I don't always eat downstairs,' he said as he left. 'If I'm working I have a tray. I'm working at present. You may join me or eat orthodox – take your choice.'

'I will go downstairs,' Georgia chose.

She lingered over the meal, imagining Mr. Smith, Agrippa Smith, upstairs, eating, probably, in anything but a leisurely manner, taking the meal in the same decisive way as he took life, and that was something that had to be done, and so accordingly was done. He would have a very regulated mind.

So different from Justin ... (why, years after, was she thinking of Justin? Was it because Cyprus had been his – their place?) ... who had been impulsive and always prone to change his mind.

She smiled over the times they had started off to the beach but finished instead in the mountains. She had liked that, it had been fun not to know one's final destination. And yet, she thought, there was one destination I did want to know; one I even believed I knew. I was wrong.

Where to select a villa? she thought next. Charming Kyrenia with its mountain backdrop, its blue water frontage right to Turkey, its English air? Paphos also with water aspects, only less sophisticated, more addicted to pelicans and donkeys? Smart Nicosia? Central Limassol?

The more she thought of it, the greater a village appealed. There were numerous charming country hamlets full of quaint whitewashed cottages, in the case of Lefkara, the lace town, blue-washed; there was Pissouri, surely the top of the world, or so you believed once you had climbed there; there were old stone castles, remnants of another era, on the southwest coast. It would be rather fun discovering *the* one. Also, she might even awaken some enthusiasm in the boys.

She decided she could eke out her coffee no longer, and, getting up, she wandered out to the front of the Curium Palace. Curium Palace was the hotel's correct name, and she allowed indulgently that there was something palace-like in its architecture, its white and gold décor, its proud row of flagpoles up which the suitable national flag was hoisted whenever some VIP arrived; on international occasions every flag.

Cyprus summer nights were breathtaking, she recalled with a quickening of her heart; there was a magical lightness in them you did not seem to experience elsewhere in this Mediterranean; even the stars threw fluted shadows on the ground, the moon cast a solid wedding-band-gold beam. A little intoxicated with it all, breathing in that herby carob-pod air she so well remembered, Georgia sauntered down to the harbour.

The open-air restaurants were fast filling up for the night, the white-clad waiters darting across from their kitchens on the street side with unbelievable loads on their trays, which they manipulated cleverly through busy traffic. Kebabs, which were skewered meat, enticed the hungry, long bottles of beer and wine gathered in the thirsty. There was either laughter, chatter, or an occasional snatch of song, but always the basic soft wash of the Mediterranean against the stone wall.

'I presume you would have taken coffee.' Someone joined her in the stroll. 'So I won't offer it. But will you join me in some Aphrodite? Ah' . . . with a small laugh . . . 'easily seen you're not a newcomer, you know what to expect.'

'Yes,' she agreed with Mr. Smith, for it was Agrippa Smith who had joined her.

'Is that yes, I will drink wine with you, or yes, I know what Aphrodite is?'

She decided that it would be rather nice to sit by the waterfront, become part of that festive setting as you sipped the deliciously fruity white island wine, so answered, 'Yes.

33

To both.'

'That's what I like,' he commended, 'a girl who knows her mind.'

He found a seat at the Mimosa collection of tables, and soon glasses and a long cool bottle waited in front of them.

'Are you similarly single-minded in the matter of our future accommodation?' he asked, lifting the bottle and pouring her a glass.

'You haven't given me much time,' she reminded him, 'I only learned your wishes some hours ago.'

'But surely something at once clamoured within you? Some favourite spot? Some place with an association?'

'No.'

'Yet you were here before on Cyprus?'

'Yes.'

'And have no association?'

She felt her cheeks reddening; although he had selected a seat away from the gay lights she felt sure the colour must show up like a flag, for she was very fair.

He gave an amused small laugh, and she realized that he had noticed.

'Then somewhere connected with the association?' he suggested.

'Mr. Smith, you may be assured I'll try to select a place suitable to both you and the children.'

'How practical we are!' he drawled.

She ignored that 'we' this time, but she did question his 'practical'.

'Why not?' she pointed out. 'After all, you did go to some pains to tell me you were a factual writer.'

'You really mean never a romantic one. But I also told you, Miss Paul, that I can write anywhere, even a place of memories, your memories – it would have to be yours, for I have none here. So please be guided by your heart, if it pleases you, it's all the same to me.' He topped up her glass.

'How long exactly were you in Cyprus?' he asked rather abruptly.

'My sister-in-law told you,' she reminded him rather shortly.

'So she did. A summer, I think.'

'Yes.'

'I believe they're long summers.'

'Six months, sometimes seven, or even eight.'

'That's sufficient time to get to know a place.' He had taken out a slim gold case and offered her a cigarette. As she shook her head he took and lit one for himself.

'Are you keeping the pipe for the boys' amusement?' she asked idly.

'If the boys are amusable,' he shrugged.

'I thought I'd take them villa-hunting with me.'

'By all means. But first we must find you a car.'

'The agents will drive us to any available places.'

'With your own transport you can delve into unexpected corners. Do you know the Greek for House Vacant?'

'They write up a sign in English: To Be Let. No, I only know good morning, Good night and *eho, ehis, ehi* ... I have, you have, he has.'

'*Eho* ... I have ... about as much.' Georgia was to learn later that this was not so. 'Incidentally,' he said lazily, 'the verb to love is very much like my own name. No' ... with a grin ... 'not the Smith part.'

She found she could recall that, and nodded. '*Agapo*, I love, *agapas*, you love—' she began.

'*Agapa*, he loves,' he finished.

He also finished the wine, as she refused more, then sat back and regarded her. The regard went on for so long that she knew she was flushing again.

'Are you always like this?' he asked.

'Like what?' she stammered.

'Man-shy.'

'I'm not! I mean—'

35

'Then it's an act?'

'It's nothing of the sort.'

'Then it's I?'

'Mr. Smith, you may be a factual writer, but you do have a vivid imagination!' she snapped.

'Those flushed cheeks are not my imagination, believe me.'

'What else can you expect,' she said a little angrily, 'when you sit back there just staring at me?'

'Oh, so you noticed that?'

'Of course I noticed, and – and it was embarrassing.'

'Don't tell me we have that rare species, a bashful girl?'

'I'm not used to being stared at,' she complained.

'Then either you are unaware of the men or they were blind, for you're a very beautiful girl. That, incidentally, comes from a factual writer.' He said it all so coolly she could not possibly gather for herself a compliment from it. It was a statement, never an award.

How different from Justin, she recalled, Justin who had paid her the most lavish compliments, his eyes affirming what his lips said, and how she had gathered them to her. She had believed they had meant that—

'I think,' Agrippa Smith's voice broke in, 'that you've more or less withdrawn from the scene for some time, hence the current blush. What was it, Miss Paul? The usual reason for withdrawal?'

'What do you mean?'

He looked at her a little impatiently, impatient at her apparent obtuseness. 'A jilt?' he suggested.

'No.' She said it so promptly she knew it must sound the opposite. But it hadn't been a jilt, she hadn't been jilted, she had just been an inexperienced young girl, who had seen more in something than had been intended. But she could never tell this man that.

A silence grew between them, a silence, she knew angrily, that spoke for itself as far as he was concerned. She wished now she had never accepted this post. She did not like, nor

ever could like, this person. The children pulled at her ...
all children did ... but they, too, offered a stormy passage.
Cyprus itself, redolent of everything that had been romantic
and beautiful, offered it, too, in its relentless reminder of
One Summer. No, she should not have agreed. Perhaps even
now—

'I've been in touch with my solicitor regarding your
employ,' Agrippa Smith said almost as though he had
guessed the progress of her thoughts. 'The papers have been
finalized,' he informed her.

'But not signed.'

'Certainly signed. Signed Georgia Paul.'

That fact came back to her in an indignant rush. This
man saying resignedly: 'Beggars can't be choosers,' then:
'Will you write your name there, Miss Paul?'

'Is it your custom to obtain a signature first?' she inquired.

'You should have checked,' he reminded her mildly. He
drained his glass, called for the bill, then got up. 'A stroll
round the waterfront?'

'No, thank you.'

'A nightclub? I'm told Limassol can supply these.'

'No.'

'Then—?'

'I'll go to bed.' She started along the promenade, then
politely, though reluctantly, she turned. 'And you, Mr.
Smith?'

'I'm not an early bedder, but I'll return you to the
hotel.'

'No need, Cyprus is a very woman-safe island.'

'All the same I will return you, possibly go up myself, put
in a few hours' work.'

But after she had gone to her suite, then crossed to the
window to look down, Georgia saw him emerging again,
emerging into the beautiful night, the summer-remembered
night, and she found an odd restlessness in herself.

37

She went to bed, as she had said, but it was some hours before she slept.

The next morning she did not make the mistake of asking the boys whether they would like to look at houses with her, she knew that their, probably a stock answer to everything, would be: 'Not much.'

She crossed to the larger suite in time to help the hotel maid . . . Katarina, she was told, by that smiling Greek-Cypriot girl . . . to finish dressing the boys.

'Such good boys,' said Katarina, who had some English, 'I say to them "If you sit still while I pull on the *fanella*" . . . the undervest, madam . . . "Katarina will find you some *siokolata*." '

'Chocolate,' nodded Georgia. She smiled at Katarina. 'I think they answered when you asked if they would like that: "Not much." '

'Yes,' said Katarina, puzzled. 'Such good boys, though, not to need—' She sought for a word she needed.

'Bribe,' suggested Georgia with a secret sigh. She looked at the neat little boys. 'Have they had breakfast?' she asked the maid.

'Yes. Also taken their little pills.'

'Vitamin dragees,' came in Bish blandly. 'To supplement our diet.'

Katarina looked a little confused, but Georgia, accustomed by now to the boys' sophisticated vocabulary, was glad she had been informed. She had been considering asking their father if he thought their bored outlook could be the result of some vitamin lack, but now she wouldn't.

'Multi,' went on Bish, 'also iron and calcium.'

On an irresistible impulse Georgia asked, 'Do you think it benefits you?' and waited for the yawn or the 'Not much'.

'If you don't take them you're not dead, we know that, because we tried spitting them out for a week and we were still alive.' It was Seg.

38

'So then you took them again?'

'Our mother wished us to.'

'That was nice of you, then.'

They both said together, and seemed to consider it was an end to a discussion, so Georgia accepted that finality: 'We don't see her much.'

'If you're ready now,' she said, 'we'll call in on an agent. This agent has houses to let, and he'll take us around in his car.' To any other children, she thought, she would need to add: 'Please behave yourselves,' but there was no need here.

'We've gone round before looking at houses,' said Bish.

'In agents' cars,' said Seg.

Georgia wanted to say: 'Boys, is there anything you haven't done before?'

But if they did not enjoy themselves, though on the other hand they did not noticeably dislike the procedure, they simply remained the same, Georgia enjoyed herself immensely.

The high ceiling price that Mr. Agrippa Smith had allowed her allowed the agent to expand himself, and they examined villa after villa of the better class, beautiful houses with sweeping views, enclosed courtyards, in some instances ... and she had been influenced by this until she noted Bish's and Seg's bored little countenances when they saw them ... swimming pools. Georgia took down particulars in a notebook and said she would let the agent know.

As they drove back into the city, the boys in the rear seat, Georgia beside the agent, Georgia wondered if an apartment might not be better, for that pair behind her needed none of the villa advantages supposed to be afforded to children as opposed to flat living.

They had been examining some offerings out of town, and now the agent's car swept back in the direction of Limassol, skimming over the spectacular hills above Happy Valley, where, though the heat was dazzling, Rugby was being

39

played at this moment by some ardent R.A.F. teams, then past the point to the Queen Mary Hospital.

'Stop,' directed Georgia abruptly. 'Take the Plantation Road.'

'It is a little longer,' demurred the agent.

'I know, but ...' Georgia leaned out. She was remembering this road clearly ... barley fields running into an aquamarine sea ... Kolossi Tower looking down from its stony height ... bruise-blue mountains pondering over it all ... then far above the carobs trying to climb those mountains the first of the flamingoes flying south. She and Justin had been privileged to see that lovely thing, see that unforgettable rose-pink flight to the shallow salt lake at Sovereign Akrotiri, where they gathered every year before they flew to Nairobi. Afterwards, Justin had rimmed the lake, and the flamingoes had rested there, only faintly pink in relaxation.

Justin had talked about Kenya, where he went regularly, and its Rift Valley where the flamingoes congregated in thousands, and the way he had told her had made her think that the next time he went she would be beside him ... but evidently, biting her lip now in embarrassed memory, she had not said, as she had said at Bellapais, any 'our', any 'us', for he had not become silent, and she had not guessed *why*.

'Why,' came in Seg from the back seat, 'are we stopping here?'

'There are no villas,' observed Bish.

'There were flamingoes,' Georgia explained.

To her surprise they did not know about them. More surprising still, they tacked on to that admission a curious 'What are they?' So they were not entirely lacklustre.

'Birds – wading birds, very lovely birds. They're pink.' She saw that flight again, that rosy necklet in a blue Cypriot sky.

'Why do they come here?'

40

'To rest on their way south to escape the winter. From the Camargue, perhaps, in France, where there's a colony.'

'I want to see them.' It was Bish, and for the first time Georgia saw a flicker of interest in him. A pity, she thought, that the annual flight was long over.

'I'm sorry, darling.' She nodded for the agent to go on.

When they returned to the Curium Palace, Agrippa Smith was standing in the avenue beside a small smart car. Georgia thanked the agent, told him she would do some considering, then turned to tell the boys to alight, for they were not the usual little boys who leapt out first.

But today they had leapt out, and she put it down to the new car, an attraction to any old or young male, until she found that they had bypassed the car and gone into the hotel.

At a nod from Mr. Smith, she crossed to his side.

'Your transport,' he indicated.

'It's new.'

'Any objection?'

'No . . . except . . .'

'Frightened you'll inflict the first scratch? Not to worry, I'm a believer in things being used. It would be almost impossible, I should say, not to drive around this island without gathering a few dents.'

'I won't look for them,' she promised, 'and though a used car would have done, still thank you very much.'

'How did you fare with the agent?' he inquired.

'I've taken a lot of notes for you.'

'Nothing jumped out? No bells were rung? No house suddenly opened in-beckoning doors?'

'No,' she said a little stiffly. 'If you'll read the notes—'

'Not now. Nor tonight. My publisher is flying in on his way to Jo'burg. There's to be a brief conference up at Nicosia. I'm leaving at once and won't be back until tomorrow. Can you hold the fort here?'

'Of course.'

41

'Then here are the car keys, go where and when you please. Even though you've contacted an agent, afterwards you may care to look a second time; also often an unescorted tour will produce something new.'

'Yes, you're right. Thank you, Mr. Smith.'

He nodded briefly, turned to a chauffeured car that he had evidently ordered, for it was now drawn up at the kerb, then got in and left without another word or look.

Georgia went in, too. Examining places to live in was a rather exhausting business, and she ran a warm bath and soaked for a long time. House? Apartment? She considered each in turn. The house seemed likely to win, not because of the boys, for if ever children were apartment-slanted children those two were, but because ... well, an apartment seemed more exposed, more – more intimate. She felt she could not live in such a place, however large, with Mr. Agrippa Smith. In a villa you had patios to escape to ... gardens ... courtyards. You had a better chance of not running into a tall, broad, pipe-smoking (cigarette at night) individual with an odd twist to his mouth and narrowed, baiting eyes.

There was a knock on the door. Georgia was inclined to disregard it, until it came again ... again.

'Wait, please,' she called, then got out of the bath, dabbed off the surplus moisture and climbed into a towelling robe.

She went to the door and opened it a bare inch. When she saw Katarina there, she opened it further and told the maid to come in. It would be concerning the boys, she thought, probably refusing to eat supper. Certainly it would be something of that sort, never anything actually naughty.

But it was naughty. More than that, it was alarming. Katarina was alarmed. Her big black eyes were swimming with tears.

'The two children,' she wept, 'they are not here. More than that, they have left the hotel. That small Bish and Seg, madam, they are gone!'

CHAPTER THREE

THE first thing, Georgia told herself, was to placate Katarina; these Cypriot women were very tenderhearted, very emotional. If she showed the girl the concern she was feeling, for one had to be concerned, even this soon, about children, she could start a panic.

Telling her to go back to the suite, that the boys might be playing jokes with her ... jokes? that pair? ... she dressed quickly, then joined Katarina in the apartment across the passage.

'They run in,' related Katarina at once, 'so I go down to the kitchen for milk and biscuits for them, then when I come back ...' She spread her hands in despair. 'I look everywhere. I know boys, I have brothers of my own. Under beds, behind doors, in cupboards. They are not there, not anywhere.'

'They'll be in the garden.' The hotel had attractive surrounds.

'I have looked.'

'Then up the street, along the by-pass. There's a toy shop, and you know what children are.' — But not these children, Georgia thought bleakly, not these probably toy-saturated small humans.

'The desk did not see them go out,' fretted Katarina. — Oh dear, Georgia thought now, I hope she didn't make too much of it when she asked.

'They would creep out the back way, through the kitchen.' A little desperately, trying to convince Katarina, she repeated, 'You know what children are.'

'They are good boys, never naughty ones.' As before, the girl looked a little puzzled over that.

'I think,' lied Georgia, 'in fact I'm *sure* I know the

very spot.'

'Madam can find them?'

'Yes. And they certainly would have returned themselves in time' . . . she tried to make it airy, casual . . . 'but all the same, I'll go and collect them.'

'Yes, madam, do. Mr. Smith set me to look after the small ones, and when they are not here to look after I am anxious.'

'All a storm in a teacup,' Georgia reassured her.

'What do you say, madam?'

Georgia remembered a piece of old Cypriot wisdom Justin had told her; Justin had been a keen folk scholar, undoubtedly wherever he went he had soaked himself in the country's lore. This Cypriot saying had been: 'If you don't say boo in a well, it does not respond boo.' Meaning if you do not start trouble, you will not be troubled. She said this now to Katarina, and the girl smiled her understanding at once and became composed again. As she left her fussing around the room, Georgia thought gratefully of Justin and his Cypriot sayings. She remembered other sayings from Justin . . . some from Nairobi, Nairobi to where the flamingoes flew south when they left here. She wondered why in her present trouble – for, away from Katarina, she had to admit it was trouble – that that had occurred.

She got into the new little car, in her deep absorption not worrying about the familiarity or otherwise of gears. Before she realized it she was out of Byron Street and proceeding along the port road at such a snail's pace that anyone would think she was either a learner driver or unsure of her direction. In actuality she was straining her eyes from right to left for a glimpse of two small boys in blue shorts, white shirts and sandals. Where did little boys go? That was easily answered. They poked around the water . . . but not on this occasion, she saw, knowing, too, that she would have been surprised had she seen that pair there. The balloon-seller? No, she had offered them balloons once today and they had been supremely bored. She looked up to the giant figure in the park advertising the Wine Festival, and remembered how small boys were fascinated by his size and how they stood beside him trying to measure up their own height. She had stopped the car, and now she walked into the Gardens. But no small boys, or at least *her* small boys, rewarded her.

Perhaps in the attached zoo. She looked in vain. The aviary. She looked again, and though in vain not so much in vain as before. For something had begun to nag at her. Bish. Bish showing his very-first-interest-ever. Bish asking of the flamingoes: 'What are they?' Finally: 'I want to see them.'

It was a long shot, but that very-first-interest-ever could not be pushed aside. Georgia went back to the car, got in, released the brake, then began the journey to Akrotiri, thankful that Cyprus summer days were long, and that she could expect bright sunlight for some hours yet. She did not point out to herself the absurdity of two little boys covering the considerable distance to the salt lake, for knowing these little boys now, she knew she could expect anything this amazing from them. *Suspect* anything. Suspect that the empty taxi that had just passed her had not been empty on its forward journey. Had she thought of it quicker she would have stopped the taxi and asked the driver if two small people had driven out with him from Limassol, for although they were only six and seven that was exactly what that sophisticated pair were capable of.

And, she saw, rounding a bend, actually had done. For there they squatted in some meagre brush beside the now dry lake, two little boys, Bish and Seg, and . . . and she could not believe it, not this long after migration, not four months after as she remembered from her last time . . . a flamingo. Just one flamingo, and flamingoes went in large flights. It wasn't true, it couldn't be true, but there they were, two boys and a slender pink bird.

She came carefully across and sat down quietly beside them. It gratified her more than she could have thought possible that they accepted her without question, did not even consider it necessary to put small fingers to their lips for silence. She knew ... and glowed foolishly because of it ... that in this moment she was one of them.

She watched them watching the bird, not taking their eyes off the bird, absorbed, engrossed at last. Engrossed for the first time in their blasé lives?

Then she, too, gave her attention to the flamingo. How, she wondered, was it still here? She supposed it must have been either too young or too weak for the flight south. Perhaps it had started with the others, fallen behind, lost its way, so came back. Perhaps it had been rejected because of its fragility, not included in the southern contingent ... oh, there were scores of reasons one could attach to that slender, beautiful thing of white and rose-pink.

But if it had been young and weak once, it appeared full-size and robust enough (if robust could ever be applied to a slender flamingo) now. She glanced around her and knew there would be worms for the scratching in the surrounds where it had lodged itself, small molluscs left over from the lake after it lost its winter-wet and became summer-dry.

But it was still a marvel it had survived; there were the inevitable marauding animals, certainly rodents, on the island, and the open season for shooting would have been still on for weeks after its companions had flown south.

Another marvel, and a greater marvel, was its calm acceptance of them. Even as Georgia watched, the flamingo allowed Bish to stroke its long down-curved bill.

'It doesn't mind you talking,' permitted Seg to her.

Georgia asked: 'Can I touch it?'

'Yes.'

She did.

'Did you come out in a taxi?' she asked as casually as she could, and they nodded back just as casually. Probably it was the sort of thing they had been used to doing all their lives, but it was the sort of thing she must stop them doing. It was unthinkable that children of six and seven could travel by themselves in taxis, unthinkable that they carried that kind of money. She was surprised that Agrippa Smith had not checked their pockets and restricted them to jingling money, not the folding variety that a trip from Limassol to Akrotiri would entail.

But— 'He was a good taxi man,' related Seg. 'When we told him when we got out that he must go to the Hotel to be paid, he said he would.'

'I see.' Georgia was glad that Mr. Smith had had the sense to restrict their wherewithal. She also could understand how the taxi man had agreed to the boys' instruction, for one look at those small, obviously expensive, immaculate children was sufficient assurance that he would be paid.

'Did you see the flamingo when we stopped here today?' she asked.

'No. But you said they came here.'

'But only in winter. Then they migrate to Kenya.' – Flamingoes flying south ... she saw that rose-pink ribbon making flowing patterns across a soft blue sky.

But one flamingo had remained.

'I'm calling him Flamey.' Bish was touching the down-curved bill again, the wading bird calmly permitting him.

'I'm calling him Rose Red Morning Cloud,' said Seg. – A future writer like his father? Georgia wondered.

She returned from the future to the present again. *Calling* him? Surely they didn't think ...

But they did.

'He's ours – we found him. He likes us. He wants us.' They must have seen the look on Georgia's face.

'But, darlings, he's a wild bird ... not wild in nature, I can see that, but wild as regards Mother Nature. I mean, he's not used to captivity, and he would be unhappy if you kept him. In the end it would be more unkind than kind.'

'How could it be unkind not to be dead, because if we leave him he'll be dead?' asked Bish in a complex way, though Georgia followed him.

'That's right,' said Seg. 'I saw a man with a gun, and in the distance Rose Red Morning Cloud could look like something to shoot.'

'He's going to be Flamey,' insisted Bish.

'He's going to be—'

'Hush,' directed Georgia, 'the pink one is becoming alarmed.'

He wasn't. It occurred to Georgia that this remarkable bird never would be. But the boys were looking at her with one look, one agreeing look. Unmistakably they were agreed.

'The Pink One,' they said in unison. 'We're calling him the Pink One!'

'Thank you, boys, but we still can't keep him, you know.'

'Why?'

'In the hotel?' she scoffed.

'We're moving,' they pointed out.

'In an apartment?' she scoffed again.

'A villa,' they said. 'We looked at villas.'

'I looked. You two never got out of the car.'

'We didn't have the Pink One.'

'We haven't now. Oh, boys, can't you see that it wouldn't be allowed? There are protection boards, and wildlife has to remain like that.'

'And get dead?' they asked.

They made sense. The flamingo had been lucky, very lucky. Georgia doubted if its luck could hold. It was so beautiful, it stood out, and to stand out in nature was to invite disaster. Especially now in Cypriot summer, that ochre and cigar leaf summer, when its colour comprised almost a rose-pink shout.

'A villa with a garden, a lot of garden,' said Seg.

'A view of the water – being a wading bird the Pink One would want that,' said Bish.

'What about his food?' asked Georgia.

'We'll dig, won't we, Bish? Also, you can drive us down for sea things.'

'Boys, I don't know,' Georgia sighed.

But she did know, really. She knew she was going to move from the hotel as early as tomorrow. She was going to select the villa now, any villa so long as it was large, had a garden, had a view of the sea, and nearly all of them had had that, would do. Meanwhile, she was going to put the boys – and the Pink One – in the back seat of the car – she had no doubt the flamingo would accept this quite amiably as he seemed to accept everything else – go to the agent, make a decision, receive a key, settle the Pink One for the night, settle the boys back in the hotel (she smiled as she anticipated a little trouble there) and—

And that was what she was going to do.

They had seen the smile. They were getting to their feet, they were carrying the Pink One carefully between them to the car.

'Do you remember any particular villa?' she called, getting behind the wheel.

'No.'

'Well, it doesn't matter,' she supposed aloud.

The agent seemed a little surprised when she said any villa would do. Being an astute agent, he chose the most expensive, but Georgia did not argue, she accepted the key and they drove off.

The house was on a hill between Limassol and Amathus; it was large, two-storeyed, white with blue shutters. It had an immense garden and it looked on to the Mediterranean. There was also a half-dry ditch in the fold of two small slopes behind it which Bish and Seg leapt at eagerly.

'The very thing for wading, for mucking about,' they claimed.

49

'It will have to be by itself tonight, you do understand that?'

They did, if unwillingly. They found an old chicken coop in a barn to enclose the Pink One, and promised him a hundred times that they would be there first thing in the morning.

'For ever and ever after that,' they added lovingly.

'We'll bring worms,' called Bish.

'And sea things,' said Seg. Georgia did not think he was quite sure what sea things comprised, but he could handle that better than molluscs.

She did not go through the house – probably she had already; she had seen so many today she could not recall any in detail, but anyway, it could wait until tomorrow. She knew it would be like all Cypriot houses, part marbled, part polished timber, to serve both the hot and cold weather. It would be gracious with many arched corridors, with many large rooms . . . and with Agrippa Smith she needed many large rooms. Rooms to go to when she wished to avoid him, for he was a man she knew she would want to avoid.

Coming out to the car, she stood a moment before she called to the boys to make their final good nights. She was looking down the hill to the translucent sea, the leaves of the olives that grew almost to the shores turning silver as a gentle wind combed through them, the regimented carobs Indian-filing their way across numerous fields with goats with silky-eared kids threading their way between the rows of gourds, a donkey so still he must be stone, a tinkling bell-wether leading a flock home. It was all lovely, yet it was not just the loveliness that caught wonderingly at Georgia. She thought: I've been up here before.

It would soon be dark. She turned and called the boys to the car.

No need to waken Bish and Seg the next morning; at first light they were banging on Georgia's door.

50

'Hush, you'll rouse all the hotel!' she scolded.

'The Pink One will be wondering where he is,' said Bish.

'He'll be needing to look around for worms and sea things,' said Seg, 'and he can't, he's in that coop.'

'The sea things have to be fetched up to him, stupid,' said his brother.

'Well, molly-cules, then.'

'Moll-uscs, and they *are* the sea things. Hurry up, Georgia!'

Georgia could scarcely believe her ears. She had told them they could call her Miss Paul or Georgia, whichever they wished, but she had not dared hope for that easy, companionable, unencumbered 'Georgia'.

It was far too early for breakfast, but she could not imprison these two here waiting for it. She decided to drive them to Amathus and leave them there. They would be quite safe – children, as well as women, were very safe on this island, and anyway, she could not see them moving far away from the Pink One. As for their breakfast, she had no doubt they would meet a bread pedlar on their way out, his hot *koullouri* steaming fragrantly in his outfit's little heated glass container.

'Right,' she said, 'but I can't stop with you, there'll be packing to do, quite a few things to see to.'

They hardly heard her, they urged again, 'Hurry up, Georgie!'

As she had anticipated, the sesame bread seller was cycling along 28th October Street. She stopped and bought a bag of *koullouri* and some *meli keik*, or honey cake. They were not interested now, they were only anxious to get there, but in time the pangs would make themselves known and they would seize on the paper bag.

Barely had she stopped the car than they were out and racing to the coop. She found herself racing after them, her heart thumping. For suddenly she knew that this was very important, important to two small boys and a larger girl. If the Pink One had escaped, if the Pink One had met with a disaster, she might as well pack her bags.

Then: 'Hullo, hullo,' she heard Bish calling joyously.

'How are you, my friend?' called Seg.

Georgia did not know she had been crying until a drop ran into her mouth. Then she laughed.

'There's a bag of sesame rolls when you feel like eating them,' she called.

'Mm,' they nodded.

'I'll go back now. I'll be as quick as I can.'

'Buy a spade,' directed Bish. 'I think this ground is harder than the Pink One had before, so we'll have to dig for him.'

'Bring some sea things with you,' said Seg.

'That will be your job,' she tossed back. 'When we get things fixed we'll go down to the shore and find some molluscs.'

They did not reply. They were squatted down again, repeating last night's adoration. It was as good a time as any to slip away, so Georgia did.

Back at the hotel things still were not stirring, so Georgia spent a busy half hour packing up for the boys, and for herself. Though she hesitated doing it, she supposed that since Mr. Smith would be moving, too, she had better pack for him. Feeling guilty ... yet why should she? ... she went into his part of the apartment and began taking suit coats off hangers, trousers off clips. She could not do the lot, not knowing what he intended to change into, but this lot at least would help with their evacuation. She bundled out socks, very large in the feet, she noticed, pullovers both sleek and rough, a jacket with leather patches where he would wear a sleeve out writing. She held that jacket an odd moment, aware sharply of a male tang she had not smelt for years. Not since Justin. A kind of tobacco, after-shave, pencil, pepperminty smell.

'Is it in need of dry-cleaning, or are you just holding it to your heart?' His edges-filed-off Strine voice came across the room to her. He must have entered the suite and she had not heard him. He looked at the evidence of evacuation, and said: 'What in tarnation is all this?'

Georgia flushed . . . she seemed always to be either flushing or reddening before this man, a fact, she was to learn later, that also had struck him . . . and said defensively, 'You did instruct me to find somewhere to move.'

'I did, but good lord, you couldn't have achieved it in this short a time.'

'Yes,' she said.

'Even to the extent of actually beginning the change of address?'

'Yes,' again.

'But only yesterday you told me that you had merely reached a stage of taking notes.' He made his tone deliberately awed, and it irritated her.

When she did not answer, he said: 'Something jumped out at you, Miss Paul? Bells rang? A domicile opened up in-beckoning arms?'

'You are ridiculous!' she retorted.

'An old association captured you again and you signed on the spot?'

This time she did not speak, for she was remembering instead, thinking . . . and now it came fully back to her . . . of standing with Justin during one of their carefree jaunts quite near to that hill house, looking out as she had looked yesterday over translucent sea, silver leaves of olive, Indian-files of carobs, gourds lying golden in ochre fields. Just looking . . . and knowing she loved the man who looked with her.

'Aha,' Agrippa Smith pounced, 'so an association has won us a home much quicker than I thought.'

'No,' she refuted, 'it was—' She stopped. She must go carefully about the Pink One. If she burst it out, he might refuse point-blank, and what she had gained with Bish and

Seg would be gone for ever.

He did not seem to notice her anxiety. 'Well,' he said, 'out was what I wanted and I'm not grumbling because you were quicker at it than I anticipated. But why the mad rush?' He indicated the bags. 'It's not even breakfast time yet.'

'I was up, so I thought I'd attend to it.'

'Couldn't sleep, eh? Bad conscience?'

'My conscience is clear.' — Well, fairly clear, she thought; there is still the matter of your two small sons some miles out at Amathus, while I, their paid companion, or guardian, or whatever I am, am here.

'Again I have no cause to grumble,' he admitted. 'You've obviously packed for yourself, the boys, and now you are attending to me.'

'I was only doing some of your things, I wouldn't have touched anything personal.' Her glance went to a photograph on his desk . . . an oddly familiar photograph, somehow, yet she did not know why, for she had never seen the woman in the leather oval before. In the quick glance she gave it, though, she saw something of Bish, something of Seg, and knew why she recognized the likeness. It was their mother — Agrippa Smith's wife.

'Nothing personal,' he shrugged, and the careless way the photograph was deposited . . . never placed, never arranged . . . agreed with that. He would be a hard man, she thought, this Agrippa Smith.

'You never answered me,' he reminded her. 'Does my writing jacket need the cleaner's attention?'

'No.'

'Then you were holding it to your heart?'

To her dismay she heard herself answering, 'It's a long time since I handled men's clothes . . . I'd forgotten that different smell . . .' Again she was flushing.

He gave a low little laugh that made her flush even deeper. She turned to leave the room.

'No, Miss Paul, please finish. If we're to move, I'll certainly need to remove my things. Tell me about this place, please.'

He was taking armfuls of clothes from the wardrobe, dumping them on the bed, waiting for her to answer him as she folded and filled a suitcase he also had taken out.

'It's at Amathus, which is old Limassol – Richard Coeur de Lion's port. It's high on a hill ... quite nice ... a large garden ... plenty of rooms.'

'That's important,' he inserted drily, 'plenty of space so we don't get in each other's hair.'

Another flush on her part, a flush that spelt guilt, told him that she had thought in the same strain. Oh, heavens, why couldn't she control her rushing colour?

Again the little amused ... hateful ... laugh.

'Was your meeting a success?' she asked politely, folding his ties now.

'Very much so. Whatever you've promised to pay for your in-beckoning house we can well afford it.' He began enclosing his typewriter in its case, gathering up his books. 'The young fry are quiet even for them,' he observed. 'Have they fed yet?'

'Yes.' The zoo again, she thought angrily. But she felt entitled to answer Yes, since the boys would have eaten by now; the sight of the Pink One gorging on worms would have given them worms, they would sniff the cooling sesame bread and follow the smell to the large paper bag. She did not tell him what they would be breakfasting on, or where, and would not have later if it had not been asked of her, had not Katarina run in at that moment and staged the same scene as she had yesterday.

'Oh, madam, oh, sir, they are gone again! – the little ones. I bring up their boiled eggs and cocoa and what do I find? No children, none at all.'

'They're all right, Katarina,' Georgia said definitely, so definitely that the girl accepted it, and bustled out again.

But Agrippa Smith did not accept it. 'How did she mean,'

he asked, 'gone *again*?'

'They – they went off yesterday,' she faltered.

'After I left?'

'Yes.'

'Presumably they returned, to go missing now a second time. Though this time you say you know where.'

'Yes. It's the house.'

'At this time of morning?'

'They're keen on the house,' she explained.

'Well, I suppose that at least is something, that they're not entirely without interest.'

'Oh, no,' came in Georgia quickly, enthusiastically, 'not at all.'

'You intrigue me,' he drawled. 'I can't wait. But first of all, who's with them out there?'

She stood very inadequate. In bare words it must sound bad when she said 'No one', but it still had to be said.

'You mean to tell me you've left two small boys alone in the house?'

'I don't think for a minute they'd be in the house.'

'If you're trying to be funny, Miss Paul—'

'I wasn't. They wouldn't be in the house, they would be in the garden – a large garden.'

'Yes, you said so.'

'And they would be safe. Cyprus is very safe for children and women.'

'*If* they stayed there. But can you see boys staying in a garden? No, they'll be down on the motorway watching the cars, crossing the motorway to the beach. At least' . . . furiously . . . 'I hope they manage to cross without being run over.'

'They won't leave the garden,' she assured him.

'Have you tied them up? Because I don't believe the love of flowers will keep them there.'

'He will, though. The Pink One.'

There was a silence – a long silence. Then Agrippa Smith

56

said practically: 'Are you ill, Miss Paul?'

'No. The Pink One is a flamingo. It – it's my break-through.'

'Please go on.'

'They found it. It was to be Flamey, or Rose Red Morning Cloud.'

'Miss Paul, you *are* ill.'

'But I said Hush, that the pink one was becoming alarmed, so the Pink One he became.'

'I see.' Agrippa Smith's tone implied very conclusively that he saw nothing at all. 'And,' he smiled fatuously, 'he's a flamingo.'

'Left behind when the others went south.'

'And you discovered him?'

'The boys did – I told you. So we had to get a house for him. Oh, I know all about conservation and wild life, Mr. Smith, and how it's often unkind to fauna to be kind to them, but could it be unkind not to be dead, because if they left him he would be dead.' Bish had said that, and she had followed him, but could Agrippa Smith follow her?

He did – though faintly.

'He's there at Amathus?'

'Yes.'

'The boys are guarding him?'

'He doesn't need to be guarded, they're friends.'

'Have you attended to servants for the house? For provisions? For the supply of light and water?'

'No . . . but there's a bag of rolls.'

He ignored that. 'But you've attended to the establishing of one flamingo?'

'Yes.'

Another silence, longer than before, then: 'And I chose *you* to prepare these boys for a more practical life.'

'It is preparation in a way,' she cried. 'From the look on their faces I think this has been their first association with something living but not human.'

57

'And you think that's necessary?'

'Very necessary.'

There was a third pause. It seemed to go on for ever. It must preface, Georgia felt sure, her walking ticket, her way out of his employ, and suddenly, quite desperately, she wanted this job, she wanted it for Bish and Seg, she wanted it for— She gave a little start, annoyed at herself, annoyed at the way her eyes had dropped to that jacket she had held, that tobacco, after-shave, pepperminty *male* jacket.

Again she was going red.

Then she heard him saying, 'You think living things but not human are necessary ... well, so do I. What are we waiting for, Miss Paul?' He turned and went to the door.

She came after him, out of the room, out of the hotel. At a nod she got behind the wheel of the new car again while he sat beside her. She hoped she drove satisfactorily, but she would not have been surprised at anything she did.

She didn't do anything, though. She drove smoothly and efficiently to the house above Amathus.

He said as they approached the tall, white, blue-shuttered edifice: 'Fair enough.'

'It's a good view.' She glanced back at the sea, the olives, carobs, fields of gourds ... Justin. And flinched.

He was looking at her shrewdly, and she knew he would have something to say later on; little would ever miss this man.

'He's down in the fold of the two slopes. Oh, dear, I forgot to buy the spade! Then we'll have to get molluscs as well. I thought down in the bay—'

She was preceding him to the bottom of the garden, showing him the way. When they were halfway there, she ran, ran in panic. What if the flamingo had flown off, the boys run after him?

She rounded a bush and saw the same picture that she had carried away with her when she had left them – two adoring small people sitting beside a complacent bird. She went and sat herself.

'He'll come to you now, Georgie,' Bish told her. 'Just put out your hand and stroke his bill.'

'He'll try to eat your finger, but not really,' advised Seg, 'and anyway it doesn't hurt much if he does, only a sort of tickle.'

She put out her hand.

That was how Grip Smith saw her . . . and would always think of her. A pink wading bird, a pink girl. For if ever a girl could be expressed in colour, this girl was pink. Either blushing, or flushing, or reddening, or crimsoning . . . but roseate.

He stood staring, seeing the girl merge into the satin perfection of perhaps nature's most glorious bird until you could not say in certainty where the roseate story began, where it finished; you were only aware of pink.

CHAPTER FOUR

BUT when Grip Smith, having examined the house surrounds, entered the house, he was the factual world affairs
man again, no pink in him at all.

Standing nervously beside him, aware as she looked with
him that this was one of the several houses yesterday (for
there had been many, too many) that she had *not* personally
probed, that she had accepted as duly scrutinized, Georgia
became embarrassingly aware of her inadequacies in the
very first commission he had handed her.

It was a beautiful house, as many Cypriot houses are,
gracious of line, never a square where a curve could in-
terpret the need, arched, fluted, flowing. *And full of nothing
at all.*

She should have remembered that fact, she should have
recalled that a house in Cyprus 'To Be Let' generally meant
just that – only the house. Everything to make it a home
must be purchased or hired. She could only excuse her fail-
ure now in recalling this fact to seeing a little furniture in
the houses that she had examined, probably left-overs from
the last tenants. She did not look up at Grip Smith looking
down a canyon of emptiness, she looked at the floor, a lovely
glowing polished timber floor that merged into marble,
since the next room was summer-designed.

Oh, there were certainly chairs, a score of chairs, for the
Cypriots believed in chairs. They sat under trees in them.
They took them out to the sidewalk and sat in the sun in
them. They took them into fields with them as they watched
their flocks. They went everywhere. Always light, raffia-
bottomed chairs, village chairs, as they were called.

'You sleep sitting up, Miss Paul, I see.' Grip Smith's voice
came in drily. He walked into the next room to another

gaping emptiness. Another room, all the rooms. Only chairs.

'I'm sorry.' Georgia had come up behind him.

He held up his hand. 'Fortunately my financial news yesterday was good news. Take out your little black book, Miss Paul, and write down what I tell you.' Without waiting for any more apologies, he began smartly. 'Lounge: One settee, three easy chairs, coffee tables, standard lamp.'

He left the room smartly, and she had to run to keep up with him. They did not do every room, the house had more rooms than they would need, but by the time he had finished the list was formidable, and there were no drapes included.

'I could make the curtains,' she proffered uncertainly.

'Do you wish to add a sewing machine to that column?' he asked brutally.

'By hand, Mr. Smith.'

He gave a gesture of impatience. 'I don't want to wait a month for privacy, there are many windows to this house should you care to count. On the other hand, I have no intention of tacking up cardboard.' He paused, undoubtedly to let his censure sink in deeper. Then he instructed: 'Add drapes to the list.'

She did.

'Perhaps,' he said after they had finished, 'though you didn't remember that Cypriot houses To Be Let are like this, you might remember if we're anywhere near a furniture-hire shop.'

'Yes,' she said eagerly, 'a good one by the port.'

'Then come along, Miss Paul.'

'What about the children?' she queried.

'They can come, too, if you can prise them away. I don't intend making a habit of leaving them alone like this, but until I get some domestic staff it will have to be so, but what would be the use of staff without anything to be staffed?'

The children did not even consider coming; they looked

pityingly at the two adults for suggesting such an inane thing, and answered an uncompromising No. As Georgia got into the car, beside Grip this time, she started to apologize again, then was surprised by his sudden, quite unexpected boyish grin. It changed him completely. From the world affairs writer he became a chatty columnist, she thought. She would have liked to have told him so, and the present expression on his face made her think he would have accepted it.

'Not to worry,' he dismissed her apology. 'I would probably have hated the sticks, anyway. Now we can choose our own sticks.'

But sticks they certainly were *not*. Every piece that Grip Smith decided on was a very special article. When he came to her bedroom setting Georgia protested that something plain and utilitarian was all right, thank you. He brushed her words aside, and she saw a low, deeply upholstered bed-divan being earmarked, a low, deeply upholstered bedroom chair, a table with a mirror that could fit an entire room in its capacious reflection.

'Mr. Smith, I—' she began.

'Now the boys. Single rooms? Double?'

'Double room.'

'I think so, too. Beds or divans?'

'I was wondering about a double decker bed.'

'Good thinking,' he nodded. 'It could prepare them for more crowded living than their pampered years so far have done.'

They went through the whole gamut ... scatter-rugs to soften the first morning impact of marble or timber floors, office setting, dining setting, sunroom setting, bathrooms. The curtains came last, and, by mutual agreement, were plain white voile.

'So,' Grip Smith said.

They were sitting under a canopy by the harbour drinking coffee by this time, not because they were thirsty, for the very impressed furniture hirer had kept up a continual supply of drink and nourishment delivered by a small boy on a tray from a café next door, but because it had been rather tiring.

'I'd sooner,' admitted Grip Smith, 'write a chapter than that.'

The furniture was going up at once. The furniture man had been instructed where to place it. As soon as they had rested they would call at the employment bureau and obtain a cook, a maid, a gardener and an odd job boy.

'All that isn't necessary,' Georgia protested; she still felt guilty.

'I've only been on this island a short time, but I can see it is,' he refused, and she knew from her last time in Cyprus that he was right. Help was an established thing, an expected thing. Also, it turned the wheels of the republic's economy.

She became aware that Grip Smith had not spoken for several minutes. She glanced at him, and saw that he was gazing at the water, that incredibly blue Mediterranean water, the deep pure blue of larkspurs, except where it touched the horizon and changed to misty veronica.

'And to think,' he wondered sadly of the loveliness, 'that we're talking about pots and pans!'

He looked back from the water to her . . . but Georgia could not answer his gaze. All at once ridiculously shy, she had lowered her gaze. Then she looked up in shock again. 'But we didn't,' she remembered.

'Didn't what?'

'Talk about pots and pans, arrange for the kitchen. We left out the kitchen.' She half rose. He went to stop her, press her down again, then he shrugged at the water, an ironic shrug of defeat.

'If you worked on paper, it would certainly be in the domestic hints column,' he said unkindly. 'You'd go for butter always, wouldn't you, never lilies.'

'*You* say that?' she answered, incensed. 'A factual man?'

'Oh, come along,' he dismissed impatiently, leading the way across the street to the hirers once more, 'and add basins and kettles to the list.'

The cook they obtained was a man, Yiannis, and he said he understood what English people liked.

'We want Cyprus food, too,' said Grip Smith.

'Ah,' smiled Yiannis in a manner that promised future food for the gods.

Olympia was the maid, Georgiou the gardener. Georgia chose Georgiou, even though Grip Smith protested that their two names would be confusing . . . how could they be when she to him was strictly Miss Paul? . . . because she saw him talking to a dog, and an attachment to animals . . . fauna . . . could be an advisable trait with the Pink One in close settlement. Andreas was the odd-job boy.

By noon everything was delivered and everybody was there, the furniture, drapes, pots and pans, cook, maid, Grip Smith and Georgia in the house, the gardener, odd-job boy, children and flamingo outside the house. They were all kept busy the remainder of the day.

But by sundown everything was shipshape; tomorrow Agrippa Smith could sit down at his desk again and turn out concise, astringent current-affairs copy, Yiannis could cook his food-for-the-gods meals, Olympia flutter her duster, Georgiou dig around the magenta and yellow roses that ran rife in the garden, Andreas do as he was told, and Georgia take the boys down to the sea for sea things for the Pink One.

'A little browning up during the process,' advised Grip Smith, 'wouldn't hurt.'

When she asked Bish and Seg what colour trunks they would like her to buy for them . . . Mr. Smith had opened an account in one of the larger Limassol stores . . . they said pink, which, though unsuitable for boys, was still better than

64

their previous 'It doesn't matter' which they had used almost as frequently as 'Not much'. Resigning herself to some quiet persuasion for a more male and less flamingo-faithful hue, Georgia was pleased to hear Bish add that already they had swimming equipment. That was what he actually said: 'We have swimming equipment.'

She rummaged through their expensive cases and found several smart silk morsels. The labels said Biarritz. Poor little rich boys, she thought. But if they hadn't been really rich when they were rich, they were rich now. Rich in the Pink One. Their joy in that bird was a very tender thing.

It was even a small amputation to leave him to go for the molluscs, but when Georgia pointed out his need for a change of worm diet, they agreed to put on their trunks, their reason the fact that better sea things might be found away from the shore, Georgia's that their pale skins might achieve a golden glow.

She might even, and she glowed herself at the thought, teach them to swim. She enjoyed that vision. She enjoyed the idea of going casually to Grip Smith, very casually, even offhandedly, and remarking in passing: 'We had a lovely morning swimming – oh, yes, the boys swim. I taught them, didn't I tell you?'

Poor Georgia! It wasn't that they wouldn't try, it wasn't that they were unteachable. It was just that they swam, and swam competently, already. Swimming out first herself for encouragement, or so she believed, she turned round to jolly them in the water, but they were not on the beach. They were in the Mediterranean, much further out than she was, but blissfully unconscious of that fact, only concerned with:

'Mollycules!' shouted Seg, then seeing Bish's scornful expression: 'Mosaics . . . mollycoddles!'

'Molluscs, stupid. Just say sea stuff. You're a very babyish boy.'

'You're a fat pig!'

'You're a fat porpoise!'

They splashed water at each other, had they been ashore they would have thrown sand, exchanged punches, believed a surprised Georgia.

'The boys,' she reported that evening to Grip Smith, '*fought.*'

'So,' he said, and grinned. 'Time to buy some boxing gloves?'

'If you did I fear you'd find they had them already. Did you know they were good swimmers?'

'I didn't. But it would add up. The best of tuition in some posh, exclusive European resort pool. Yes, that would be Sigrid.'

Sigrid. So his wife was Sigrid. It was certainly a family of unusual names. But perhaps it wasn't unusual, perhaps she actually was Norwegian. If so, what right had the lordly head of the house to insist that their children become strictly Australian? What a man, Georgia thought, no halfway meeting where he was concerned, the woman was expected to come all the way; no wonder their marriage stood where it did.

She looked at that photograph again the next day; she had a charge plate for him to sign for her so she could use it in the store he had nominated.

The photograph was still as carelessly placed as at the hotel, as though it had only happened there, and involuntarily she went to straighten it, put it upright, more centrally placed.

'Leave it where it is.' His voice snapped irritably at her. 'Better still, take it away.'

'Away?' she queried.

'Remove it.'

'I'll put it in this drawer, Mr. Smith,' she said, 'it'll fall where it is.'

'It's fallen already,' he said.

She did not answer. This was no business of hers. But she

did give the photograph another look as she opened the drawer. She supposed it must be Bish's and Seg's likeness that made it so strongly familiar.

The boys were slowly gaining a pale honey hue. She did not know what degree of tan Mr. Agrippa Smith desired, but she was determined they would do it painlessly, which meant gradually, and helped along with lashings of sunscreen. It startled her sometimes when she realized how keenly she had attached herself to these two small people. What had been a challenge before had become something much more intimate. Instead of preening herself over her achievement with the Pink One, she found herself worrying about their future activities, for, although the flamingo seemed as content as his friends were ... Bish and Seg always called themselves that, his 'friends' ... the summer was well into maturity, some early autumn colours indeed were already showing on the Troodos Mountains, and after autumn was winter, winter when the flamingo squadrons called in at Cyprus as they flew south. This time the smaller, more delicate bird that had been rejected last year, or so Georgia supposed, would join his brothers, and if they objected, then his new strength, quite remarkably built up by worms and sea things as provided in over-lavish quantities by Bish and Seg, would afford an entry on power alone. Good for him, she thought, but what of two small bereft boys?

So she introduced Peaceful, the donkey, Buttons, the dog, Purr, the cat. She had been impressed on her last island stay at the amiability shown by one island animal to another. One expected that with donkeys, who had an inbuilt peace, hence Peaceful's name, but not with dogs and cats, yet never once had she witnessed a dog and cat fight, and it was the same with this pair, Buttons, called so since his pointer-shape torso was neatly worked in tan coins on a fawnish background, was on the best of terms with Purr, called so since he possessed an engine that could be heard all over the garden. Though not, Georgia trusted, in the library, from where Mr. Smith, since he had settled the household, had barely stirred. It was apparent that he was writing something very important, something that needed all his attention, and for that Georgia was relieved, for she did not know just how that man would take a menagerie.

She hit upon the idea of introducing the boys to future horseback riding by beginning them now on Peaceful. They looked unenthusiastically back at her when she suggested this, so to show them the ease of being jaunted around as compared to walking, she climbed on to Peaceful herself. He was a dear little donkey, with that gentle mark on him proving that he personally was related to that favoured ancestor who had carried a Precious Load to Bethleham, but he was also a donkey accustomed to big burdens, great toppling loads of aromatic herbs, lengths of timber, both usually accompanied by a human burden, with two, three, even more children. The sudden light burden that was an unencumbered and slender Georgia surprised him so much that he kicked up his heels in exuberance, and took off.

Where, oh, where, despaired Georgia, hanging on to his fortunately shaggy coat, were all those stubborn donkeys who refused to budge an inch, who had to be shoved? Peaceful needed no carrot in front of his nose, he simply flew.

At first it was fun, for the boys, anyway, and though Georgia found no fun in bumping up and down, she did resign herself to giving Bish and Seg a few moments of hilarious amusement. Then Peaceful, beginning really to enjoy himself, beginning to like the wind whizzing past his ears instead of merely settling dust on him, must have felt he would also like soft turf under his hooves, the turf he possibly faintly remembered from his small donkey years, when he had sauntered the hills at the back of Limassol by his mother's soft belly.

He turned and actually galloped, if a donkey ever galloped, and Georgia stopped being resigned to giving amusement to small boys, stopped being mildly put out by bumps, and became terrified instead. She could tell from the screams that pushed aside the peals of laughter that the children were frightened as well, frightened for her, and had she not been so scared she might have found room for triumph, a triumph that that blasé pair were worried for her.

But there was no time for anything except to hang on. Didn't this donkey know then that donkeys never move out of choice, that if they have to they proceed only by placing one reluctant foot after the other?

She told Peaceful so. She yelled it at him. And all the time they climbed, and climbed, you would not have credited that a burdened donkey could climb so fast. Then, reaching the top of a foothill, the down slope to the other side came so abruptly it took Peaceful by surprise. And Georgia. Over his head she went flying to the ground, by some miracle the donkey stepped over and not on her, then, probably scared at what he had done, he went cantering off.

But Georgia lay still.

By the time Grip Smith, summoned by two boys with an urgency he had not thought they were capable of, had got into his car and headed in the direction Peaceful had taken, Peaceful had crossed to another valley, and the landscape was empty of both donkey and girl. The ochre and pumice hills, for in summer the damson bloom and the bruisey blue of the Troodos tops either rubbed off or faded as the cooler heights descended to the hotter sea level, camouflaged everything with their nothing tone. He cursed that neutrality for its concealment, and yet, he thought, surely against the parched scene he could pick up the sight of a pink girl.

He saw nothing but the ochre and pumice, and some slender spires of thistle squills, their sky-blue tufts the only field flowers able to brave the down-soaking August sun.

Grip drove till he could drive the car no farther. He left it and began fanning the slopes by foot. He called her name. In a situation like this, you could not call Miss Paul ... nor even Georgia.

'Georgie,' he shouted, borrowing from Bish and Seg, 'Georgie!'

There was no answer. Georgia, lying where she had landed, was incapable of answering. She was concussed.

Several times Grip Smith went almost within yards of her, rock outcrop hiding her, but his calling did not reach her, and he went on.

She could not have said at what period she regained consciousness, for when a blurred awareness did reach her, she could not remember anything, neither who she was, where she was, what had happened. She just lay there.

But slowly, bit by bit, things began to unravel. She remembered thankfully from a first aid course that a skull blow that rendered one unconscious for a period could be less serious than a relatively slight blow causing no unconsciousness but having grave delayed results.

She felt confident she belonged to the first category, so after resting a while, she began to test herself, not wishing to do more damage again to a possibly damaged, if now numbed, limb. She began from her toes upwards ... wriggling the toes ... relaxing them ... making rigid the shins, calves, thighs. She was thankful that everything seemed intact.

Ribs, pelvis, stomach, all felt uninjured, shoulders, neck, back. No, she was sound, and yet she knew she could not get up.

She must get up. She had no doubt she was being looked for, but in the position that Peaceful had deposited her, she could be looked for all night. She must at least get up sufficiently to make some sign, wave a bush or something, shout.

Shouting seemed the best thing to begin with. She opened her mouth, but nothing came out.

'Help! I'm here. Help!' She said it in her mind, and

framed it with her lips, but still nothing happened.

The light was beginning to fade, so it must be some hours since she had climbed on to Peaceful to show the boys the pleasures of riding. Night would come, and though perhaps there were no more pleasant nights in the world than Cypriot night, with their barely less warmth than day, their bright starshine, she did not feel at all keen on staying here till then. Staying here for the next day. Staying here for ever unless rescue came, for she still could not move. It must be her spinal column, yet she did not feel any pain. Was that a grave sign, as the lack of unconsciousness was grave?

She shut her eyes and tried to relax. Even if I have to stay here all night, she knew, there'll be no fears of savage animals; the last lion on Cyprus was milleniums ago. She did not fancy a curious fox, though, a rodent . . . nor, looking up in terror at flapping wings, death from the sky.

But it wasn't, of course, though the shock of it did not help the state of shock that Georgia was already suffering but had not diagnosed in herself. The shock of a flamingo hovering over her, then putting down almost on her chest.

The Pink One had found her. Rising up again, the wading bird did a complete circle, then he landed a second time.

Close behind him came Grip Smith, two small boys, Yiannis, Olympia, Georgiou, Andreas, Button – no cat, since cats leave rescuing to heroes, but a repentant Peaceful, who must have returned home. All the family.

Grip Smith brushed them all back, then knelt beside Georgia. Rolling up his sleeves, he began to finger her.

'I'm all right,' Georgia said, 'I've done all that, I'm quite sound.'

He took absolutely no notice, she might just as well not have spoken; all he said was: 'Sore there? Tender here? A numbness? A pain?'

'No, no, no. *No!*' The last No was when he began to unfasten her shirt.

'Don't be a damn fool,' he said, 'I'm trying for your collarbone.'

'There's nothing,' she insisted in a quieter voice, 'but I just can't get up, somehow. Do you think' . . . tears began to roll . . . 'it's my spine?'

'It's your imagination. Sorry, I shouldn't have said that. It is *now*, but perhaps it wasn't then. When you regained consciousness, I mean.'

'And what is your diagnosis at that time?'

'Very apparent. You were shocked. Shock can keep crippling for hours, but not if it's attended to.' He nodded to Olympia, who came eagerly forward with a flask from which she proceeded to put hot liquid into a cup. When she had finished she handed it to Grip and he put the cup to Georgia's lips. The contents were extremely sweet, and she grimaced.

'Essential,' he advised. 'Drink up.'

The boys were hopping around in their eagerness to tell her something, and Georgia had a fair idea of what it was. It should have been Buttons who had led the rescue party, and perhaps given the time the dog would have, but a bird has an advantage, he can look down on a scene, and the Pink One had.

But— 'Flamingoes don't,' Georgia said faintly.

'This one did,' Grip stated, 'heaven knows how.'

'Perhaps we have a wonder bird.'

'I don't think so, I think he merely was doing a circuit, saw you and mistook you for a very large pink grub.'

'He eats worms,' she said faintly.

'I didn't like to call you that. When he found out you'd be indigestible, he just rose up again, but the kids took it for a signal, and—' Grip spread his hands.

'Factual as ever.'

'That's my metier,' he reminded her.

'Anyway, I'm thankful to him, if not thankful to Peaceful.'

'Yes, Miss Paul. About that donkey. Why was I not told

about the donkey?'

'Would you have objected?'

'I'm doing the asking.'

'Then that was why I didn't tell you, in case you objected.'

'I would think that now you wished I had objected.'

She shook her head. 'I'm unhurt. I'll get up soon.' But she was aware as she told him that that she still did not feel very able.

'Why did you do such a damn silly thing as ride a donkey?' he asked her.

'Everyone rides them here.'

'For a purpose, not for pleasure. I think this particular donkey realized that, and it was a shock.'

'There are shocks everywhere today,' she said. 'I also rode him to demonstrate to the boys the joys of horseback.'

'On a donkey?'

'You know what I mean.'

'I do. What a pity it was wasted.'

'How do you know? The boys love Peaceful, I'm sure this little occurrence would never put them off.'

'They had no need to be "put on", like the swimming,' he said. 'I'm afraid they ride well already. They have certificates from an exclusive Paris Pony Club.'

'They never told me,' Georgia objected.

'You never asked.'

'*You* never told me.'

'I didn't know until now.'

'You also didn't put your nose outside the door to find out. Your own – your own—' She had been going to say 'Your own little sons', but he intervened irritably:

'I have a deadline to meet. Good lord, what do you think I am?'

'Blind. You've employed me to prepare these boys for something that the more I see of them I realize they're better prepared for than those already there – Australia, I

73

mean.' Good gracious, she was thinking, doesn't this man know anything at all about his family?

'In other words, you don't need this job?' he asked.

She did not want that, she wanted anything but that, but she wasn't going to beg to him. 'I just mean' . . . lamely . . . 'you haven't done any homework on them.'

'Any reason why I should?'

If you can't see it, she thought, heaven help you. Aloud she said: 'I'll get up now.'

He steadied her as she did, whereupon, to her dismay, she was sick, quite horribly and embarrassingly. Olympia ran forward in sympathy, but Grip Smith nodded her away and took out his own large white handkerchief.

'Yes, shock,' he diagnosed.

The spasm passed, and Georgia murmured in a little voice that she believed she could walk now, thank you.

The 'thank you' did not quite emerge. Not only telling him she could walk, but trying to demonstrate it, she moved forward a few inches, and gave a painful little cry.

At once he was down again, and examining her ankle closer than he had examined it before.

'A Potts' fracture unless I'm mistaken. You wouldn't feel it until you put weight on it. Not a serious one, but I'm afraid you won't be leaving the job as early as you wished after all.'

'*You* wished, and I could still leave.'

'You could, but I don't wish any more, I'd have compensation to pay, even though you have only yourself to blame for this damn thing, and if I have to part out I may as well have some return.'

'You really mean I can sit while I work.'

He did not argue that. Nor did he wait to tell her what he proposed to do now. Turning to Yiannis, he instructed him to go ahead and bring the car as near to the scene as was possible. He told Olympia to go back to the house and prepare a downstairs bed. He told Georgiou and Andreas something, the boys something. Undoubtedly, thought Georgia, he told the Pink One, Peaceful and Buttons something, for he was a telling kind of man.

Just to prove that, he turned and told her what she was to do, told her by taking her up bodily and firmly and carrying her up the hill then down the slope to the car.

Here Yiannis sat behind the wheel waiting. Grip Smith got into the back seat, still with Georgia in his arms, and in that arrangement they drove back to the house.

CHAPTER FIVE

OLYMPIA had arranged a downstairs room that overlooked the garden and the hills from one window, the sea from the other. Georgia, when she protested that she could have stopped in her own bedroom, was cut short by Grip.

'You're a lightweight, Miss Paul, but I don't fancy carrying you up and down a flight of stairs.'

'I'm only very slightly fractured,' she answered. 'I could have managed, if slowly, myself.'

'We haven't had a doctor's opinion yet, any X-ray, so I don't know how gravely or slightly you've hurt yourself. But I do know that crawling up stairs would certainly benefit neither a grave nor a slight condition. What is it? Are you frightened my typewriter will annoy you? I assure you I can take it to another quarter, either that or send my work out, or even excange Old Faithful for a noiseless model.'

'Which you would hate,' she smiled impulsively. She had had a writer friend in Sydney, and she knew how attached writers become to their ancient machines.

'Yes, I would hate,' he agreed. He ran his fingers through his brown hair; the gesture gave him a rather boyish look. 'As a matter of fact,' he admitted, 'its bang is my release, if you can understand that.'

'I can. And please don't try to smother the noise. I quite like it. Any protest was because I felt I could be disrupting the family.'

He looked at her and seemed about to say something, then must have changed his mind.

The doctor came and diagnosed Georgia as a Potts' fracture case, as Grip had said.

'Doctor Agrippa Smith,' Georgia could not help saying.

He bowed acknowledgment. Yet just to make sure ... to make sure, as he put it, that she couldn't come on him for future compensation ... nonetheless he drove her down to the hospital to be X-rayed.

'You are a fuss,' she complained. 'Doctor Papademetriou saw no need.'

'Doctor Papademetriou wouldn't be called upon to support your injured ankle for life.'

'Neither would you.'

He gave a long, oddly disconcerting stare. 'I wouldn't be so sure of that, Miss Paul.'

It was a pleasant convalescence, if it could be called that, if convalescences ever are pleasant. She would lie back on her many cushions, gazing through one window at the long pale beaches edged with shining ribbons of flawless blue sea, through the other window at scattered white houses and churches with fingerpoint spires climbing the ochre foothills to plum-coloured mountains. There was a goat track curving up into the sunlight on one hill that she was resolved to follow as soon as she was able. The boys could come, too, though probably, she smiled to herself, they would leave her far behind, having been expertly trained at some expensive European gymnasium for such feats. What a complete surprise their efficiency had been ... and why hadn't their father known?

She had been speaking the truth when she had told Grip that she quite enjoyed the typewriter. Its rhythm relaxed, never annoyed her, and, punctuated by the domestic sounds in the house, the children's laughter outside the house, it all made for a rather pleasant clamour.

Only one thing intruded, and that was the future of the boys as regarded the Pink One. Georgia did worry about that.

One afternoon the typewriter stopped. Georgia was not aware that it no longer tapped since it had become such a background sound to her until Grip Smith said from the doorway of her room: 'Why so pensive?'

She was absurdly glad she had gone to the trouble today to tie a ribbon round her fair hair. She could not have said why she had done so, why she had put on some lipstick. – She also could not have said why she was pleased now.

'Come in,' she invited politely. She thought how wrong it was to invite someone into their own house, and apologized for doing it.

'*Your* sanctum,' he reminded her. He accepted her invitation, took up a chair and put it beside the deep divan bed that he had hired for her, then had ordered to be carried downstairs.

'You haven't answered me,' he continued.

She decided not to argue with him, for she *was* pensive, and it might help to share her concern.

'I was thinking of the boys,' she admitted, 'as regards the Pink One.'

As he waited for her to go on, she did.

'It's all only a little short of an obsession with them, and that's not good. Oh, they love Peaceful, Buttons and Purr, but it's the Pink One that fills their life. They associate themselves with the flamingo, and one day—'

'There'll be a flamingo flying south?'

'Yes.'

'But they will be going south, too.'

'Not where the Pink One will be going. Look, Mr. Smith, I know all of us, and particularly children, have obsessions. Teddy bears, for instance.'

'Much more concerning, I should say, for after all, a flamingo as flesh and blood is surely a more desirable outlet.'

'But a bear is there. There so long as the one who needs it embraces it. This other comfort will go.'

'Good, then. The addiction will be nipped in the bud.'

You fool, she felt like saying, with your two complex sons, made complex, I'm sure, by their complex parents, the ad-

78

diction is already in full flower.

But— 'Something else will happen,' she said instead, 'when the Pink One leaves it will be a small amputation.' As he did not comment, she went on, 'Too much obsession is never a good thing. For instance, a mother addiction—'

He got up abruptly and strode to the window overlooking the garden and the bay. 'Perish *that* thought,' he said forcibly.

She looked at him wonderingly, wondering many things ... wondering whose fault it was that these children had needed a wading bird to bring them to normal, average little people, not strictly normal or average, they were both too individual for that, and always would be, but a different story now from the withdrawn, bored, blasé beings they had been, their mother's fault in her odd upbringing or their father's fault in his absence of any upbringing at all?

What had happened to the Smith marriage? How long ago? How deep a cleft? Temporary or permanent? And if temporary, was it remedial? But most of all she wondered: Why am *I* wondering this?

He had returned to the bedside chair.

'I'm stuck,' he said, changing the subject.

She followed what he meant, and nodded sympathetically. 'Run out of thoughts?'

'That's something that doesn't happen much in current factual stuff, it can't, though just now—' He hesitated, something she had never known this self-sufficient man do before.

'I'm working on two things,' he said a little abruptly. 'I thought I'd give some copying out. Can you tell me where to go?'

She couldn't. Her brother had done his own, except when she had been here and been happy to take over the job. She told him how she had helped John, insinuating that she would gladly do the same now for him.

He brushed that aside. 'I didn't take you on as a secretary.'

Mischievously she said, 'I wouldn't charge any more.'

He shook his head. 'I'm going into town to see if I can find an agency. It occurred to me that you might like the run in, it must get monotonous lying here.'

It didn't, but she did like the idea, and said so.

He went outside to bring the car up to the door, and she slid off the divan and hobbled to her drawer for a scarf to tie round her hair. She was in the passage by the time he returned, and with an ejaculation of annoyance he came quickly forward and gathered her up in his arms.

'You damn nuisance, Miss Paul!' he exclaimed crossly.

'I'm not an invalid,' she protested.

'You would be if you slipped.'

'I have no intention of slipping.'

'Your instructions were to rest the injury for three weeks. Is it three weeks?'

'No, but—'

She could not answer any more as she was being man-handled, and not as gently as she could have been, into the car. But he did make her comfortable before he started off.

He was unsuccessful. He found no copying office, and the employment bureau had no one on their books at present desirous of temporary work only.

'It will have to be me,' Georgia smiled.

They were sitting in the car, and rather than carry her to one of the outdoor cafés, Grip had had a tray brought across to them, bearing the usual iced water as well as the thick dark coffee, sunflower seeds, grapes.

'Do you touch type?' he said unexpectedly, and she looked at him, surprised. 'A touch-typist just spins along,' he explained inadequately.

'You're in a hurry for this manuscript?' she asked.

He hesitated. 'What I really meant,' he said presently and a little awkwardly ... awkward? this man? ... 'is that in touch it's the operation and not the subject.'

'If you mean do I absorb what I type, the answer is no, or, from my training, that's what it's supposed to be. A student with an eye to becoming a good confidential secretary is strictly drilled in that at business school.' She half-smiled. 'I wasn't the gold-medallist of the year, but I got through!'

He said no more. He returned the tray, drove the long way home through villages to give her a change of scenery, then once more, upon arrival, carried her to her room.

'Thank you,' Georgia said.

There was nothing more on the subject until the next day, when, once more, Grip Smith came to Georgia's door.

'May I?' he asked. He walked in and stood beside the divan.

'I'm taking you up on that offer, Miss Paul.' At her puzzled look, he said a trifle offhandedly, 'The typing offer. You'll be remunerated, of course.'

'Then I won't do it. It's too absurd, Mr. Smith, I'm not doing anything as it is.'

'You are by being here.'

'But that's nothing constructive,' she objected.

'I'll be the judge of that. About this typing—'

'I will not be paid for it!' Georgia insisted.

'I want it done, so I'll agree to that. Do you think it will tire you to sit up?'

'My back isn't injured.'

'I could fix up a table, a suitable chair.'

'Mr. Smith, there's nothing wrong with me!'

'You can have a stool for your foot.'

'If it will satisfy you,' she nodded, 'I'll agree to that.'

'You see,' he explained, with a lack of composure she had never seen him betray before, 'I've done this thing, and – well – well, I'd like to get it in typescript for my second checking. I could attend to it myself, but I've a current affairs deadline to meet.'

'Please yourself which you give me,' she told him.

'I do the current affairs direct on the machine,' he informed her. 'When it comes to facts my fingers are an extension of my brain. But when ... well ...' He was actually fumbling a little, she saw.

Presently he said, 'I've two machines, I'll bring you the lighter of them, you wouldn't be a banger like I am.'

'Very well,' she agreed.

He fixed up the table, fixed up the chair and stool. He checked his writing with her to see if she followed it without trouble. She did. It was surprisingly neat writing for a large person. She assured him there would be no worry.

'So you'll be able to spin through.' Once again he spoke a little oddly.

Georgia expected he meant speed through it, and she nodded. After he had left, she estimated the length to be that of a smallish book, more a novelette than a novel. She slid in the paper and began.

She was a good typist, but she had not, as she had told him, graduated as top of the school. She had liked her job for the freedom it gave her ... no preparatory work after hours as for teachers, no sudden calls as for nurses ... and she believed she had schooled herself to be fairly mechanical in her execution. Not as much as some, she had seen girls type every word, every punctuation mark, yet still not lose one second. – 'You must read copy, not absorb it,' her teacher had told her. 'There must be no contemplation.' She resolved to do this now.

She typed all day, quite enjoying being useful instead of an ornament, enjoying time speeding by instead of having to be filled in.

The neat pile of typescript grew. Georgia reckoned she was halfway into the book. Then— Insiduously, the theme, the tune, the mood of what she was typing seeped into her. She paused, and turned back a few pages ... turned back a few pages more.

Then she had the manuscript on her lap and was reading it, not just reading it to copy it, but *reading it*. Feeling laughter in her . . . feeling tears . . . feeling something secret and haunting and very lovely. For that was what it was: a love story.

'So you don't just type.' Grip Smith had not waited to be asked in this time, he came in and took the manuscript from her hands.

'I'm sorry,' she stammered.

'It's my fault, I should have known it would be impossible for you to copy and not absorb.'

'It isn't impossible, I do it. But—'

'But?'

'Somehow this came through,' she faltered.

'You really mean you were curious what I was so anxious about, so you probed.'

'I mean nothing of the sort. It just – well, reached me.'

'And since then you haven't stopped laughing.'

'What do you mean, Mr. Smith?'

'The factual Agrippa caught up in the web of love. What a joke!'

'You're wrong,' she protested.

'I was wrong believing a female when she assured me she'd do what I asked and nothing more.'

'I tell you I never had that idea.'

'On the other hand,' he ignored her, 'I should be flattered that you took that much interest in me, enough interest to probe.'

'I didn't probe!'

'But you read the damn copy, didn't you?'

'Yes, I did. Or some of it before you came in. Do you want to know what I found?'

'No, I don't.' He took up his manuscript roughly, then turned to go through the door. Suddenly and angrily he came back and took up the pages she had completed and tore them across.

'You'll be recompensed,' he snapped.

'For what? I was only filling in time.'

'All the same, you put in some hours you wouldn't have otherwise.'

'It was a diversion.'

'And an amusement?'

'Oh, for heaven's sake, Mr. Smith, how temperamental can you get?'

That hit home. She saw the dull colour creeping up his face. After a while he said, 'I suppose I am a fool.'

'You are,' she assured him.

'Forget the whole thing.'

'You're the boss,' she shrugged.

'And that's how you consider me?'

'Of course. How else?'

He looked at the book, at her, then ran the tip of his tongue round his lips. She saw he was about to say something, and felt herself stiffening in anticipation, feeling that sensation one received when one is going to hear something that is important to them.

'Georgia.' She had been concussed when he had called 'Georgie' that day, so she had never heard anything from him when it came to names other than 'Miss Paul', so she looked at him in surprise.

There was another pause, a pause of preparation, *his* preparation, then Bish's voice cut through the waiting, cut sharply and anxiously.

'It's the Pink One, the Pink One ... Georgia, Grip, Olympia, Yiannis, Georgiou, Andreas ... the Pink One!'

The wading bird was certainly in a bad way. At first Georgia thought he had been attacked; one wing hung useless, he was bleeding. Because his balance was affected by the damaged wing, he veered drunkenly to one side. She felt tears filling her eyes. Beautiful pink bird, how had he come to this?

Georgiou, who had an intense love of animals and birds, was saying savagely that he would get that cruel shooter, but

Grip, who had been looking objectively at the flamingo, said it was a landing injury, no bullet, no marauder of any sort, that the bird had inflicted it upon himself. He was, after all, Grip said, for all his maturity now, through circumstances not long on the wing, inexperienced in fact, and evidently he had misjudged.

'He found Georgie.' It was Bish, defensive for the Pink One and his flying ability.

'Yes, he did well there, but today he spiked himself.' Grip was approaching the bird carefully, extending his fingers to it, soothing it with little comforting sounds.

Amazingly amiable, even in its distress, the flamingo allowed him to take him in his arms and examine him.

'Shall I have Georgiou and Andreas fix up the coop so as he can rest?' asked Georgia.

'No.'

'But he'll need to be confined to regain his strength.'

Across the pink and white bird, Grip caught and held Georgia's eyes, held them unmistakably, held them significantly.

But you can't let him die without trying first, Georgia's own eyes said back to him.

It would be cruel to try, flicked his. It would be against nature. I'm going to do the only kind thing – take the children away. Don't make it harder for me.

No!

Do as I say.

No.

Even if he recovered he would be miserable.

We don't know for sure, do we?

Georgia, stop this nonsense.

NO! No words had been said during all this, but their eyes fought it out, the others watching silently.

Then Georgia said aloud: 'Andreas, rig up the coop. Olympia, bring a bowl of warm water and bandages. Bring rags. Bring tapes.'

She turned challengingly to Grip Smith, but he had gone. Well, that was better than still fighting her, but she could have done with his co-operation. There was to be none. She heard him get in his own car that he had bought and leave the house on the hill in a hurry. Probably in a rage as well. All right then, if that was how he wanted it . . .

She permitted the boys to remain with her so they could soothe as she worked on the damaged bird. He was a remarkable one, she felt sure at times she must have hurt him, but not once did that down-curved bill lift to attack her back.

Georgiou and Andreas were fixing the old coop, making a floor of clean sand, putting in bowls of water. Because they badly needed something else to do, something more positive than soothing, Georgia directed Bish and Seg to find food, and, as soon as they had run off, settled herself to the more serious task of taping the bird up.

It took a long time, and she was not aware that the sweat was running down into her eyes and that her hair was soaked, until a handkerchief mopped her brow.

'Right,' said Grip Smith, 'lay off now, the expert is here.'

'Expert?' she queried.

'The aviary curator has sent up his best bird man. Step back while he gives his opinion, but I can tell you now, if it's negative, as by all bird law it should be, I'm not listening to you any more.'

Georgia saw his reasoning, if sorrowfully. You could not sentence this lovely thing to a caged life, and if it was to be crippled, a cage would be essential for its preservation.

She stepped back.

The bird man was examining the flamingo closely. He took his time. Then he got up.

'Well?' asked Grip. He said to Georgia: 'Mr. Stephanides . . . Miss Paul.' He waited while they exchanged courtesies, then: 'Well, Mr. Stephanides?'

'It is hard to say. These birds are never domesticated birds.'

'This one is,' Georgia said.

'Perhaps there could be recovery, but what kind of recovery?' Mr. Stephanides spread his hands.

'We could wait and see.'

'No,' came in Grip, 'that would be cruel.'

'You have to give him his chance,' Georgia cried.

'To be half alive?'

'On the other hand,' came in Mr. Stephanides, 'he could be a fully recovered bird. As I said, it is hard with an instance of his size to estimate the extent of damage, it could be that it is more superficial than we think.'

'He would have to learn all he has learned alone, and laboriously I should say without any example, all over again,' said Grip.

'He would do it—he's a very special bird,' fought Georgia.

'We're getting nowhere,' Grip said. 'I don't want to destroy the bird – good heavens, it's the last thing I could want, but I don't want to preserve it for a coop. Not that lovely thing.' He paused. 'Flamingo flying south,' he said, and Georgia saw the Pink One with him, in roseate flight to Kenya.

'It could be this way, it could be that,' said the bird man, and he made a balance scale of his arms.

'The children—' appealed Georgia.

'Would suffer more than if we finished it all now.'

'If it has to be, which we don't know, even the expert doesn't know.'

'Oh, girl, girl!' Grip cried.

'For the bird's sake, for the Pink One's sake, give him a chance,' begged Georgia.

He stood silent.

'For my sake,' she said.

Now he looked at her, and Georgia knew she had never really been looked at by any man before in her life. Never by

Justin. This man seemed to be looking right into her. What was he seeing? she thought, suddenly startled. Then she heard him speak. He said the words gruffly.

'All right, then. For your sake.' He turned to Mr. Stephanides. 'What is to be done?'

The man made a gesture. 'The lady has taped the bird as well as I could tape it. Rest is all that is needed now. After that the usual recuperative things, the usual offerings to sick bird . . . some green food, perhaps, even though ordinarily the diet does not include such variety. Cuttlebone might be advisable. No allowance of any mite infestation. But most of all rest.'

'How long?'

'For general health, not long, I think. For wing recovery, as long as it takes the bird.'

'Thank you,' said Georgia.

They carried the Pink One to the coop and settled him there. Grip Smith drove the man back to the aviaries, and Georgia sat by the coop talking softly to the bird.

One thing, she thought, as the sun went down and it started to get dark, there would be no need to worry about warmth. The night air would be little cooler than now.

Olympia came down. She looked worried, so Georgia told her not to be sad, everything could turn out all right after all, they had just to wait.

'But those boys,' said Olympia, 'there are not here.'

The boys! She had forgotten all about the boys! The last she remembered was settling them to the job of finding food for the flamingo. That had been just before her taping of the bird, the taping that had taken all her attention and a great deal of time.

'They'll be down in one of the gullies with the spade. Tell Andreas to go down to call them home.'

'He has been, madam.'

'But they can't have gone far, they would be too anxious about the Pink One to leave him. Unless . . .'

Yes, unless . . . And that was what they would have done, gone down to the beach for 'sea things'. In their anxiety just worms would not have been enough for their 'friend'.

Forgetting her ankle, Georgia rose sharply, then as sharply drew in a painful breath. She had re-wrenched the wretched thing.

Her little intake of breath came at the same time as Grip's car up the drive. To her relief, even in her pain, two small boys got out . . . but oh, what a mess! Not just a muddy mess, but a bloody one; they must have fallen on the rocks, for they were scratched and torn.

She could see that Grip was furious. That unaccustomed father had a lot to learn, she thought.

He turned on her, and called, 'All right, you're so clever with birds, see what you can do with two little fiends who crossed the motorway and then promptly fell over a cliff, and don't try to defend them by saying they meant well.'

He said the last words to himself, though; the pain in the barely recovered ankle was sharper than it had been on its first infliction, and Georgia felt herself pitching forward. Well, was her last thought, I'm glad I'm not vomiting this time – anything but that.

When she awoke she was in bed in the divan, properly in bed . . . she wondered a little about that . . . and there were two other beds in the room; it was a regular ward, you could say.

Sitting in the middle of the room with a book and a pen to write with, no noise from a typewriter to disturb the patients, was Grip Smith.

He saw Georgia open her eyes.

'*Doctor Smith's Ordeal*,' he said of his open pad and poised pen, 'how does that sound?'

'Your new book?'

'Yes.'

'What about *Doctor Smith's Decision*?' she considered.

'I made it long ago,' Grip Smith said.

CHAPTER SIX

To make it easier for Olympia, they kept it a ward until the patients were moving round again. To carry meals upstairs as well as down when the three plates could be put on the one waggon and wheeled in together would have been an imposition, Grip said, and he was heartily agreed with. Georgia for her part preferred the boys with her; they diverted her, and lately, for a self-sufficient, independent person, she had felt a need of diversion, while the boys . . . well, it was quite apparent that the boys were becoming fond of Georgia.

Apart from a few deeper cuts that could become septic, Bish and Seg had got off lightly, their worst punishment had been the removal of oil which had drifted in to that particular beach, and which Olympia, not knowing of any easier way, had tackled with scrubbing brush and soap. The marks of her vigour still showed. Adding to this a few stone bruises, an emotional exhaustion over the Pink One, and you had two small boys not so unwilling to be confined to bed as was time-honoured with small boys.

Georgia's ankle, if not as bad as it might have been, was certainly put back for a few days.

'That will larn you,' Grip Smith leered.

'I think you're enjoying all this,' she grumbled.

'I am. I have the three banes of my existence cooped together in a manageable bunch. What more can any disciplinarian ask?'

But the disciplinarian was only bark, and even then at times the bark was reduced to a woof. Times like when Grip Smith walked in with colouring books for the boys, flowers for Georgia, and an elaborate Pirates' Den, An Amusing Game for Up to Four Players for them all.

'It says four players,' Bish pointed out as Grip started to go out again.

'That means not five or such,' explained Grip, 'it means nothing over. Up to, it says.'

'We're not four,' Seg backed up his brother.

They both said together, 'So you'll have to play, too.'

If she had not been a little unsure of the disciplinarian, Georgia would have giggled outright. The thought of the world-known current affairs writer Agrippa Smith sitting down to a child's game sent bubbles of mirth tickling through her, longing for release. Only by pretending deep interest in something out at sea did she prevent his glowering gaze on her. As it was he looked furiously with her, and remarked, 'I can't see anything.'

'It's gone.'

'If it was ever there.'

'Grown-ups talk funny,' Bish said. 'A blue counter or a green, Georgie?'

'Give her pink,' said Grip.

'I've given you red.'

'Suitable,' inserted Georgia.

'And white and yellow for Seg and me. Yes, you do talk funny. Cry funny, too – no wet. The first one to throw six begins.'

It certainly was an amusing game, but the trouble, as far as 'funny adults' were concerned, it was also an endless game. For just when you thought you were Home, or only needed a nudge to Home, you threw something, and instead:

'Pirates' Den

'Begin again!' yelled the jubilant boys.

The third time it was too much for Agrippa Smith. He got to his feet and made almost drunkenly for the door.

'As father material,' called Georgia acidly, 'you're not.'

'Then it's just as well I discovered that in time,' he called back, and shut the door on her, his sons and the game.

'What did he mean?' asked Bish.

She could not say that for the period when he took them to Australia it would be schools, guardians, trustees, house fathers . . . anything but the father he should have been, but wasn't.

'He was just talking, darlings.'

'Like I said, grown-ups talk funny. Only not you, Georgie.'

'Aren't you grown-up, then?' inquired Seg.

I don't know, she could have answered them. Sometimes I feel a wise woman, but sometimes I still feel eighteen, and standing on a hill . . . with Justin. This very hill on which we are situated now.

Seg was rearranging the counters, the game was commencing again. Georgia felt a stab of sympathy for Grip. Still, it was better than brooding over the Pink One, whose fate still hung in the balance. All the faithful Georgiou could report was that he was still resting quietly.

'Eating?' asked Georgia.

'Not yet. But that will come, my little hares.'

Georgia felt as each hour . . . for they demanded hourly bulletins . . . brought no negative report, that the Pink One would pull through, but to what extent? She shrank, as Grip had, to pronouncing a sentence of imprisonment for the basic sake of existence on that lovely pink thing. Born free, she grieved, but man decreeing differently.

There was no second participation on Grip's behalf in the dice game, and once convinced a fourth was unnecessary, the boys did not care. But Georgia cared; she felt that a father had lost an opportunity.

However, the typing began again, the quick bang of the current affairs copy. She had come to differentiate the two works now, the slower tempo that often resolved into thoughtful silence when the book was being composed compared to the extension of brains-to-fingers process when the political data was being snapped out.

Only when the boys slept did she take out her thoughts of the book she had half typed for Agrippa Smith. She remembered the laughter, the tears. The tenderness. Remembered *with* tenderness. She wished she could tell him how she had been moved by the manuscript, but how could you tell a stony-faced man who would not even find time to know his own sons? Anyway, by the hard snapping typing, *that* manuscript had been put aside.

Then the following afternoon the typist arrived and was introduced.

She was English, and spending her vacation on the island. She had heard a lot about it . . . she had paused a moment . . . so had decided to see it for herself. She had secured Limassol digs, but living was expensive, so this offer of a temporary job was most welcome. She could tour around, yet still not deplete her savings. She was delighted . . . thrilled, was what she said . . . to accept a post with *the* Mr. Smith. She said it. Her eyes said it. All of her said it. And it was a very pretty girl saying it.

'She's prettier than you, Georgie,' Bish said frankly.

'She's pretty like our mother,' Seg submitted.

They both looked Georgia over, then agreed that she was more like the Pink One.

'Pretty?' angled Georgia hopefully.

'No,' they said unanimously. 'But it doesn't matter, just like it doesn't matter with the Pink One now he's ill.'

Somehow, for all the brutal truth, Georgia felt a glow. Though the glow lessened somewhat when the typist carried in her morning coffee to drink it with Georgia.

The boys were quite wrong, Kate Elway was not just pretty, she was beautiful. She had dark gold hair, as contrasted to Georgia's tow . . . fair was a kinder word . . . and violet eyes. A girl with violet eyes, thought Georgia, has everything. She was a little older, she judged, several years perhaps, but then Agrippa Smith was young-old, or old-young, whichever you preferred. But why, angry with herself, had she thought of Grip Smith?

But it was soon obvious that the conversation was to be all Grip Smith . . . or nearly all.

'He has a wonderful brain.' – Only the brain? Georgia found herself asking – 'Have you read *Conquest in Our Time*? . . . *Portraits and Policies*?'

'No.' Besides violet eyes, thought Georgia now, this girl has a superior intellect.

'Only what I'm on now is totally different, so different it's hard to believe the same man has written it. 'It's . . .' Kate searched for a moment . . . 'quite haunting.'

'I'm sure.' What an intelligent response, Georgia squirmed, angry with herself. 'I'm sure.' She waited a moment, then slipped in, 'Actually I believe Mr. Smith was after someone who would type and not absorb.'

'One could not *not* absorb this book, it seeps into one,' Kate said. 'Anyhow, I'm not the kind of typist who has to turn over the pages and read, I get every word as I work.'

Which I couldn't do, remembered Georgia, or anyway didn't do. I put it on my lap and read it, and he saw.

But for all Kate's superior brain, superior typing ability, superior lots of things, most of all her violet eyes, Georgia could not help herself liking the girl. She was friendly, unassuming, gave Georgia a fellow feeling in Georgia's sensing of something in her life, too, that she did not want to speak about, and she was easy-going with the boys.

The boys were up now, still wearing bandages here and there, and one wound on Seg's leg was receiving antibiotic treatment since it looked slightly septic, but hale as ever, and simply crowding the Pink One with their over-attention.

Georgia, hobbling round herself, followed them down to the coop once, and was worried at the unceasing talk with which they plied the flamingo. They didn't talk as though he was a bird, they talked as though he was a brother, and Georgia was concerned.

She told Kate over the coffee break ... it would have surprised her had she realized how many times she did tell things to Kate, what confidantes they had become ... and Kate had laughed: 'Not brothers, Georgia, brothers fight, and much more healthy, I'm sure.'

'Well, you know what I mean.'

'I do. And I see your point. Why aren't the children at school?'

'They're very intelligent, I don't think this break is doing them any harm intellectually.'

'That's not the point ... though you do have a point there all the same. These kids with their private personal expensive tuition behind them – for it would have been that, I suppose—?'

'Undoubtedly,' Georgia said.

'—Would be several telling grades ahead of their age group, not a good thing for any kids. But' ... a craft smile ... 'not in a Greek school where they would have a language hurdle to hold them back.'

'A Greek school?' asked Georgia.

'Why not?'

'They can't speak Greek, except a few words picked up from Andreas and Georgiou.'

'Good, then, at last we find something the nice little horrors don't excel at. We send them to school, and besides finding their own level they learn the language as a language should be learned, from the natives themselves.'

It made sense. It made such good sense that Georgia could have cried with frustration that she had not thought of it herself.

To drive home her inadequacy even further, Grip Smith seized on the idea with deep admiration for Kate.

'Kate, Kate,' he cried, 'where would we be without you?'

'The boys haven't agreed yet,' Georgia smugly. She could not see that pair agreeing, indeed she could see them objecting strongly, and though she knew it was a good idea, and though she knew it would be beneficial all round, she could not help herself meanly anticipating a first-class rebellion.

Poor Georgia!

Called to their father's side, after he had explained their fate to them, instead of saying 'No, thank you' ... 'We won't go, I'm afraid' ... 'We're busy just now' ... typical polite Bish and Seg replies ... they said:

'Wow!'

Georgia would not meet Grip Smith's taunting eyes.

'You can find a school for them,' he told her meanly. She thought angrily that he mentally prefixed it with: 'Just for that, Miss Knowall, you can now make your contribution.'

She took the boys with her in the little car, resentful at them for their excited chatter, for their letting Kate know, if unwittingly, what they needed ... but not her.

They found a small school in the foothills that took in infants, a Greek school but with an English-speaking Greek teacher who was delighted to accept two English children.

'Australian.' Georgia almost had said Strine.

'*Poli kala*. Very good. It will be good for all of us, I think, my little fellows. You think so? Yes?'

'Yes.'

'Yes is *Ne*.'

'*Ne*,' they called.

They started at once. They didn't even look back at Georgia as she went down the school path to the car again. She got in, released the brake, then went back up the hill.

Halfway there, she pulled the car into a small safety ramp, the same ramp she recognized as the one she and Justin had used when they had driven up to look over Amathus. The road to the house had been restricted to them then, not as it was to Georgia now, so they had terminated their journeys here.

She looked back at the larkspur, the veronica, the almost cardboard cut-out perfection of the Mediterranean seascape, the paler-than-light light of a Mediterranean day clipping everything out in sharp relief. That was something, she thought, the boys would find different; Australian distances swam dreamily in blue haze.

She turned to the hinterland, to the smaller pines of the foothills, that grew into tall ranges, rustling and swaying in a slight breeze that barely stirred their bigger, stronger brothers. She recalled Justin choosing one young tree and she choosing another and timing them to see which moved the most. They had done a lot of foolish time-wasting things like that. Yet had it been really time-wasting? Did you need always to be stuck at a typewriter to fill in life profitably, not just profitably as regarded comfortable returns, but other kinds of returns?

She turned back . . . and gasped.

A car had pulled into the ramp behind her. A man was getting out. Three years were tumbling out with him. Three years ago . . . with Justin . . . on this hill.

'Justin!' She looked at him incredulously, the same Justin, not a day older, not a day different. Not a day less dear . . . less remembered.

'Georgia!'

He was racing across. He was spinning her up in his arms, something he had always done when they had met and there had been no one around to smile. She recalled significantly, though it had not struck her significantly then, how Justin had always chosen his times. It had been because – and she had been too inexperienced to see it – he wanted no involvement, nothing more than what was happening now.

'Still a featherweight, still a thistle in the wind,' he laughed. She had yearned once to be a tall, gracious lady, and he had said, 'Pixies just now are suiting me very well, thank you.'

She had not asked what he meant by 'just now', she had

97

rejoiced in the fact that he liked her as she was. How terribly immature she had been!

Yet at this moment he was telling her she was still the same.

'Only—' he added.

'Only, Justin?'

'I'd like to say "Only attainable", Georgia, but I don't know, do I?'

'Know what?'

'I can't see any ring, either wedding or engagement variety, but there could be something.'

'There's nothing,' she said. 'But' . . . flushing, she always flushed . . . 'I was always that.'

'Attainable?'

'Yes.'

He looked at her gravely, mutely asking her forgiveness. 'I wasn't,' he said.

So that had been the story, that had been the reason, when she had said 'our house', that he had left the words poising there.

'Oh, Justin,' she cried, 'you could have told me.'

'I know. I know I should have. I know I should never have let it get that far. But you were so sweet, you were so vulnerable.'

'I doubt if it would have hurt as much as not telling me. Were you married then?'

'Good heavens, no. But I was engaged. – The date was set.'

'And now, Justin? Your wife is with you in Cyprus?'

'No.'

'She never came?'

'We never married, Georgia. When we met again, Katherine had changed her mind.' He gave a little hunch of his shoulders, a habit of his, she recalled.

'Tell me about you,' he urged . . . he seemed not to want to talk about what he had just told her.

'I stayed on with John till he was finished,' she related, 'then we went back to Australia, John got Munich—'

'Yes, I know all that – reps do get to know each other's moves.'

She nodded. 'You went to Athens . . . then—'

He recited a dozen places to her. One was Nairobi.

'Where the flamingoes go,' she murmured.

'Yes. You should see the Rift Valley when the pink contingent takes over. I'm to return there to finish off a detail I omitted after I conclude here. Perhaps you'll come too, Georgia.'

'With you?'

'With me.' He paused. 'Come properly. Come as my wife.'

'Oh, Justin,' she said half crying, half laughing, 'that was years ago.'

'It's as new, as fresh and as real as if it was just now.' He turned round to look out at the blue and veronica. 'It is *then*, isn't it?' he said after a pause. 'The calendar hasn't turned at all. We loved this hill. We'd try other places, but always we'd return to the hill – our hill. You must have felt, it, too, Georgia, for you've returned now.'

'I haven't really, I'm going up the hill. I live up the hill.'

'In the hill house?' They had often discussed the hill house and wondered what fortunate person lived there.

'Yes. I work there.'

'What kind of work? And why are you here in Cyprus . . . I mean apart from the reason I can hardly bear hope it is, Georgia . . . you did say you returned to Australia?'

'And became a career girl, until John and Leone asked me over, and I accepted the invitation.'

'To Munich, but that's not Cyprus.'

'Neither was Thessaloniki, where we had a holiday together, and where I decided John's wife was becoming just a little child-worn. So I kidnapped her to Cyprus for a week, and at the end of that week I got this offer of a job.'

'You haven't said what kind of a job. Not housekeeping, are you? Who owns the house?'

'I don't know. Mr. Smith is hiring it – he is the Agrippa Smith of current affairs volumes.'

'I know of him, of course. Some man. And you're typing for him?'

'No, Kate is.'

'Oh,' said Justin, and Georgia thought she heard a relieved note, 'there is another girl.'

'Yes. And a very beautiful one.'

'Good. Very good. I've seen photographs of Smith, he's a good-looking man as well as a brains trust.'

Georgia shrugged.

'You still haven't told me about the job,' he reminded her.

'Two children. Boys,' she explained.

'Smith's?'

'Not that you'd notice,' Georgia said bitterly. She gave Justin a general idea of the situation.

'Well, I'm not a father myself,' he admitted, 'but it does seem a little raw. However, a man with a brain like his should be forgiven a lot of things.' Justin spoke with admiration.

'You mean be permitted facts before people?'

'You're really bitter, aren't you, Georgia? What is it? Does he mean more than a talking topic to you?'

'The boys do. And he puts his wretched current affairs in the boys' place.'

'Without his current affairs,' pointed out Justin fairly, 'I would say there wouldn't be much of a place. He must make a fortune on those books.'

'But to put facts before—' she started to say, then stopped. For one book had not been facts, it had been – a love story.

'Funny little Georgia,' Justin was intoning. 'If the man

spent the time you consider he should on his sons, then the shekels wouldn't come in for the sons. Be reasonable, darling.'

Darling. The word came out instinctively ... and it stopped there. It stopped between them as they stood on the hill, the ochre and cigar leaf slopes on one side, the blue and veronica on the other.

'Gigi ...' Justin said. The old name, the old loving name was brought out again.

'Why are you here?' She pushed in the words before he could go any further. She wasn't ready for anything yet.

'*Up* here? You know, don't you?'

'In Cyprus.'

'It's come round again, it's my turn, I mean.'

'For how long, Justin?'

'The same as before.'

'Summer—'

He nodded. 'Maybe a few months over, but *summer*. I had a free morning, so I came up the hill for a reminder. A reminder of another summer, Gigi.'

'It's over,' she sighed.

'If it's remembered it's never over. Look, I have to get back to work. I think you're returning to the house.'

'I've placed the boys in a school,' she told him.

'You'll be taking them every day?'

'It's a long walk.'

'I wasn't asking that, I was asking—'

'Yes,' she said.

'Then tomorrow?'

'Justin, it's over.'

'Not while it's remembered. And you have remembered, because you drew up your car here, as I did. You've remembered as I have.'

'There needn't have been remembering,' she said a little bitterly.

'I was engaged to be married, Gigi – did you want a man

who would walk out of a promise?'

She thought a moment. 'No . . . no, I suppose not. But, Justin—'

'Let it rest now. Go up to the house. Bring your children down again tomorrow, collect them . . . but some time, Gigi, stop, stop and remember. And if I've found the time between my trade calls to come and remember, too, get out of the car and remember with me. Is that asking too much?'

'Oh, no, Justin.'

'Go now, little one.' – He had often called her that, called her little one. 'I have an appointment for which I'm late already. But don't forget to remember . . . and don't forget to look.'

He waited while she got back into the car and finished the run up the hill. As she turned into the drive she saw his car joining the coastline traffic back into Limassol.

She went into the house. She could hear the typewriter tapping, by the quick efficient ring she knew it was Kate at work. What was she on, she wondered, current affairs – or a love story? With someone as practised as Kate, the speed would not alter. Kate had no need to take a manuscript in her hands to absorb it, she could type and let it seep in at the same time. She had said so. Was she doing it now?

A little irritated – though she knew she had no reason to be, the girl was simply better than she was, better in every way – she went down to the coop and sat and talked to the Pink One.

'Soon . . . soon . . .' she crooned to the lovely bird. 'Just a little longer and the sky is yours again.'

'What's this?' Grip Smith had joined her. 'You put the kids to school because you want the bird free from intrusion for a while, then you promptly intrude yourself.'

'I wasn't intruding,' she protested, 'I—'

'Then tell me what sitting beside a coop and talking in that tone of voice comprises if it's not intrusion.' He peered at her closely. 'Also looking like that,' he said.

'Looking like what?'

'Pink.'

'You're always remarking on how I redden,' she reminded him coldly.

'Not redden, grow rosy. You are now. What's happened, Miss Paul? Did the kids' teacher knock you off your feet, for of all Greeks, I hear, the Greek-Cypriot is the heart-throb fatale.'

'Likewise the female?'

'I'll let you know,' he promised.

'No,' she said, and could not have told why she retorted it sharply, 'let Kate know.'

'I shall, Miss Paul.' He still stared at her. 'You've grown pinker,' he said then.

Georgia got up. She knew it had been silly coming down and talking to the bird when that had been the reason that she ... no, it had been Kate, Kate who did everything so perfectly ... had suggested school for the boys. But that intimate tap of the typewriter had angered her. She had resented Kate taking up what she had not succeeded in doing. She had had a mental picture of them there in the study, Mr. Agrippa Smith, famous writer ... Kate, the violet-eyed girl.

'Do you like violet?' To her horror she had said it aloud.

'Considering changing from your own colour?' he asked lazily. 'You were extra pink just now and you didn't tell me why.'

'A goatherd serenaded me on his reeds,' she cried, 'a bell-wether rang a little bell song of love.'

'How nice for you, and how convenient to be a liar. Something happened. You have a glow.'

'You mean, I suppose, my nose is shiny. Why aren't you factual like your books?'

'Not all my books are factual. There is one, you may recall ...'

'You tore it up,' she reminded him.

'Kate has typed it again.' He paused. 'It was about Kate I wanted to speak.'

'Violet.' She only semi-murmured it, but he heard, pieced what she meant, and smiled.

'Yes,' he said, answering her previous question, 'I like violet. What man wouldn't?'

What man *couldn't*, Georgia thought . . . when the girl was a girl like Kate?

'It's ridiculous Kate paying the rent she does while we have room to spare here,' he began.

Georgia did not comment.

'So I'm considering telling her to relinquish her Limassol apartment and move in,' he said next.

Georgia still did not comment. He waited an impatient moment, then asked a little testily: 'You have no objection?'

'It's not my place to object.'

'Agreed, but after all, children come before a typewriter, and you as their watch-girl—'

'Oh, so you think that?' she pounced.

'Of course I think you're their guardian – I should do, I pay you for it.'

'I meant you do consider that children come before a machine.'

'Yes, Miss Paul,' he said with deliberation, 'I think that, and for that reason I'm doing you the courtesy, as a specialist in this matter, or so I trust, of asking you first.'

'And if I say no, don't bring her here, what then, Mr. Smith?'

To Georgia's complete surprise, he answered at once, 'She doesn't come, of course.'

It took all the fight out of her. She looked at him in bewilderment. Probably he was laughing at her, but he seemed serious enough.

'Well,' he asked at length, 'what do you say?'

'Of course she must come. Anyway, the boys like her.'

'I've noticed that.' – I bet you have, Georgia thought.

'Also,' he went on, 'she makes some good suggestions regarding them. The school, for instance.'

Georgia nodded. She's smarter than I am, she thought, and – and she has violet eyes. Oh, how stupid can you be? She got up and kicked at a stone.

'Don't do that,' he said sharply. 'I've been watching you lately, and you're not as sound yet on that foot as you should be.'

'It's all right,' she assured him.

'It's not completely recovered. In which case I propose to leave you in the room you're in now, not impose upon you the burden of the stairs again.'

All this was coming to something, Georgia thought, and in the next minute she learned what it was.

'Kate can have the room you had upstairs,' he went on.

'The boys?'

'I'll leave them downstairs, too. Don't want to make you feel deserted.'

'No,' she said faintly. She was thinking of her old room, not the size of it, which was inferior to her present room, not the aspect, which was not as good ... but the graciously arched hall that led to a string of rooms on the same upper level. The end room. His room. Grip Smith's room.

All upstairs.

CHAPTER SEVEN

GEORGIA carried her things down that she had not bothered moving during her convalescence and arranged them round the room that would now be hers until she left Cyprus when Grip Smith left with his sons for Australia. Upstairs, she heard Kate placing her own things. Grip had taken Kate down in the car to collect all her belongings, then he had gone with her to the agent to return the key. Kate now officially belonged as much as Georgia to the house on the hill.

While they were away, Georgia had picked up the two boys from school. After their cheerful acceptance this morning, she had not expected them to be exactly tearful, but she had anticipated perhaps a certain note of doubt. There was none. They both were radiant. The called '*Kalispera sas,*' which she knew from the remembered summer, and now this one, was 'good evening', but added a deal of childish chatter that she could not follow.

'What was that?' she asked.

'Talk.'

'What did it say?'

'See you tomorrow ... you bring the ball, we'll have Andreas carve out a bat.'

'And to that little girl,' pimped Seg ruthlessly, 'Bish called out—'

'I didn't so!'

'You did!'

'Fat donkey!'

'Hairy goat!'

'Get in, both of you,' directed Georgia, and began the drive up the hill again, glancing instinctively, in spite of herself, at the safety ramp.

'We must have our hair cut,' Bish said ... the two did wear their mops rather long.

'The other boys have their hair very short, one boy's is shaved. I think I'll be shaved,' said Seg.

'Another thing,' directed Bish, 'no more lunch from Olympia, we want sesame rolls from the bread man — all the children have sesame rolls.'

'Very well,' agreed Georgia.

'How was the Pink One?' they asked.

'I think he missed you, but the rest would be good for him.' She did not tell them that she had 'intruded', as Grip Smith had put it.

'There are still lions in the woods,' said Bish. 'Zavallis said so.'

'Who is Zavallis?' she asked.

'A boy at school.'

'Is that his name?'

'His second name — Georgie, you are childish today.'

No, you two have grown up a little today, Georgia could have said.

'Do you call each other by second names?' she asked.

'Of course. Boys do.'

She wondered what all the Eleftherious and Pierides and Markous thought of Smith.

'There are no lions, not for thousands of years,' she informed them, dropping a gear.

'Zavallis saw one. He thinks it had eaten a goat or a donkey.'

'Or a shepherd,' added Seg.

'Anyway,' they both said in relish, 'it dripped blood.'

Monsters! Georgia thought, turning in at the house.

The boys had raced at once to tell the Pink One all that had taken place, and for want of something to do, oddly restless, unsure of herself, Georgia wandered after them.

It was ridiculous, but the flamingo seemed to be absorbing every word they told him. She knew that they really believed he did. It would have to stop soon. It would have to stop, anyway, before migration time came round again, otherwise the boys could be right back where they had been when she first had taken them over. She could never picture them waving good-bye to their 'friend' without suffering some major emotional amputation.

On the other hand, would the flamingo ever be capable of leaving? Its health had improved rapidly, but Georgia was unsure of its spirit. Several times she had crept up on it and seen it nervously opening those beautiful wings, lifting the head with the down-curving bill as it looked cautiously at the calling sky. Poor, lovely, earthbound thing, perhaps Grip had been right, and this should have been decided promptly in the beginning. Yet how . . . *how* could they not have given the wading bird its chance?

She was not aware that the boys had run off down the valley, where they had a favourite digging spot, and had left her alone by the coop again, until Grip Smith, pausing an unbidden moment as he always did, and he was angry with himself for it, to gaze at the pink girl beside the pink bird, called: 'You're as obsessed as the boys. Haven't you anything better to do?'

Thinking he was censuring her, Georgia flushed, hating her inevitable warmth as it flooded her cheeks, knowing it must show out on her fair skin like two flags.

'I'm sorry, Mr. Smith,' she said quietly, 'have you a task for me?'

'Foolish child!' He was annoyed that he had spoken like that, annoyed that she had taken him seriously. 'I was joking, of course. You're doing a task just being here. I told you so before. I presume the kids are worm-digging.'

'Yes.'

'How did they get on today?'

'Quite remarkably. I should say they'll have two languages very soon.'

'You're wrong.'

She looked at him quickly at that, her heart sinking, for he must mean that he was curtailing the Cyprus stay. She did not want it to end yet. Because of the boys she didn't want it. Because of herself. Because of— well, because of Justin. Because of—

But she brushed that furiously aside, wondering why it had rushed so unerringly into her mind.

Grip Smith was lighting his pipe. 'They already have three,' he observed laconically, 'so I see no reason for loud hoorahs for a fourth.'

'I suppose so,' she nodded, vastly relieved that it was not all over yet. 'I forgot they were small jet-setters.'

'Jet-setters' progeny . . . well, one side, anyway,' he said caustically.

A few minutes went by in brooding silence, then Grip proffered, 'When I said what I did about having something better to do, I was referring to your spare time, Miss Paul. For you must have relaxation periods, otherwise the island employment board will be after me.'

'I'm not Cypriot-employed,' she pointed out.

'Then the English opposites, and they'll probably be more severe on me still. You've only to blab—'

'I wouldn't!' indignantly.

'I know you wouldn't, because you're not getting the chance. You're taking proper, legal, duly recorded days off. I've had Kate type out an official form.'

When he had begun talking, Georgia had opened her mouth to object. She loved it up here in the hill house, just driving the boys to school, doing a little Limassol shopping on her way back, just wandering round the garden, staring out at the blue and veronica, at the cigar leaf and ochre, was all she asked, but when he had brought Kate into it, she had stiffened. Of course, she thought. He wanted her away. Not indecisively away as she would be if she was still around the house, but the definite absence that presumably went with a prescribed stand-down period.

'Two full days a week,' he was saying, 'and I mean full.'

'Yes,' she said tonelessly.

He waited a while for her to take up the topic, but as the while grew into a long while and she made no comment, he shrugged a little irritably.

'Well, see to it, will you? Choose your days, either consecutive to give you time to run round the island, see what you might have missed before' . . . a little pause . . . 'or punctuated breaks to get the kids out of your hair.'

'They're never in my hair,' she assured him.

'I believe you. Anyway, they'd slip right out. What is your hair made of? I've wondered several times. Corn silk?' He put up his hand and touched her head, and the touch reaching through to her scalp did strange things to Georgia.

'I – I'll let you know.' She got up abruptly, stood indecisive a moment, not knowing where to go, then turned and ran down the slope to where the boys were digging.

'Easy on Potts',' he warned after her. There was a note in his voice she could not sort out.

Georgia did not see Justin for several days. She always looked as she came back up the hill from school, aware that her heart was thudding and her hand ready for the brake. But after the third morning she only glanced to the ramp, and thought that if it kept on like this she could forget that she ever had met him again. Already the meeting was a little dreamlike.

Then on the next day she turned the corner and the car was there. He was coming . . . running . . . to meet her.

'I've been at the other end of the island . . . I couldn't let you know . . . it was hell being as close as an island must make you yet still not be with you, Gigi.' He put his arm around her waist.

'No, Justin.' She withdrew.

'But why? And, Gigi, I don't mean why because up here no one can see us, but why can't I? Why can't we? I have no strings. You haven't. There are no promises behind me. This time it's clear sailing, and I want you with me at that helm, darling. Georgia, I mean this. Marry me.'

If only he had said that in that remembered summer! She was not aware she had cried that aloud until he reproached her, 'But you wouldn't have had me go back on my word?'

'No,' she said miserably, 'you did the right thing, Justin, the only honourable thing.'

'Then?'

She fidgeted . . . yet what she wanted to ask him had to be said.

'Justin, was it Katherine's choice, or yours, that you are now unmarried?'

'Katherine's,' he said honestly.

'Then if she'd wanted to go through with it—'

'I would have – I told you so, Georgia. It was right and honourable.'

But that was not what she needed to know, she needed to know had he wanted it more than not wanted it . . . she needed to learn had she and Katherine stood together and he had to make a choice . . .

But she couldn't ask. She turned her head, but in her confusion she turned it to him, not away.

He kissed her. She stood a moment in that kiss, not sure of how she felt. Then, pulling away, she went back to the car and up to the hill house.

They met several times, but never did Justin kiss her again. He always had been very intuitive, she remembered gratefully, he had never spoiled a moment by a wrong word.

Grip Smith did not speak again about her stand-downs, but he must have directed Kate on the matter, for the secretary came with a roster she had made out.

'How about Tuesdays and Thursdays, Georgia?' The

violet eyes smiled at her.

'They're schooldays,' Georgia pointed out.

'I could run the kids down.'

You could do anything, Georgia thought, but it was not so jealously thought as knowledgeably. Kate was very efficient.

She often listened to the two of them, Grip and Kate, in the office across the passage from the room that was now permanently hers. She did not mean to listen, but she could not help but hear the low amicable easy conversation, not the actual words but the equable tone of them. They got on very well, she knew.

'Any days will do, Kate.'

'Days,' smiled Kate. 'Plural. You're a glutton for work.'

'You're the same yourself.'

'Perhaps. It fills in time.'

And you have time to fill ... as I have ... Georgia was sure of that. She had guessed from the first that there was a remembered summer somewhere back in the years, too, for Kate.

'Those days will do, then,' she said, 'Tuesdays and Thursdays.'

'Good girl!' Kate hesitated, almost as though she wanted to sit and talk to her, talk woman's talk, not whatever went on in the office, not observations of the boys, but heart-to-heart things ... then she smiled again, she had a lovely smile, and went back with her roster.

Georgia had not seen Justin for several more days, but she knew it was to be expected; though not a large island Cyprus was a comprehensive one, there was much to visit, in a rep job like Justin's much to do.

On her first stand-down, she drove the car to Nicosia and visited the smart shops there. But her next break found her surfeited with smartness, and wanting the simple life again. She had Yiannis pack a picnic lunch, took out her bathers and went down to the coast, rimming around it in the small car until she found a suitable beach. This was not difficult; the coast was literally fretted with inviting bays and reaches. most of them since school was in term quiet and empty. The only low mark Georgia could allot were pebbles instead of sand, but she did manage to find a fairly smooth section, made smoother still by a small boat ramp that had been scraped out. She selected a large concealing rock and changed.

She did not swim at once. She lay in the warm sun, letting its golden comfort sink deliciously into her skin. Then, almost intoxicated by it, she ran into the water to let the soft waves waken her up, but finding the temperature barely cooler, so delightful indeed that she turned on her back and nearly fell asleep afloat.

She opened her eyes with a start. There was the chugging of an engine too near for comfort. She saw a small motor boat coming towards her, and only just managed to dive underwater in time to escape being run down.

At once the engine was cut, and almost immediately she heard a splash as a figure dived in beside her. She surfaced. The person who had dived from the boat surfaced. They surfaced within inches of each other . . . and laughed.

It was Justin.

'Thank heaven you're all right!' he said between splutters, for the laughter had nearly drowned the pair of them.

'Did you know it was me?'

'No, I was bringing the boat in when I saw a blob of red to the port side – your cap. I thought I'd run you down.'

'So you saved me.'

'It wasn't necessary. Look, we'd better carry on this conversation aboard. There's not much tide movement just now, but *Blue Girl* is getting away from us.'

'Is that her name?'

'Yes, but I'll be changing it to Georgia.'

'That's nice of you.'

'Shut up talking, honey, and swim across. You can, can't you?' He said it confidently, for he knew her standard from the remembered summer, knew that she could handle herself in the water.

Side by side, stroke by stroke, they swam across, and once there he scraped aboard, then, leaning over, he scooped her up. In the boat he did not release her at once. He held her loosely, yet his eyes held her tightly. Although there were some inches between them as they stood in the slightly rocking *Blue Girl*, their wet bodies clung.

'Sit down,' Justin said a little gruffly. 'Didn't anyone ever tell you not to stand up in a boat?'

'You. Many times.' She laughed at the memory. The boat had been the *Heron* then, and he had moored it at Kyrenia.

'Is this yours?' she asked.

'I was giving it a trial run. Why I happened to come here I'll never know, but I can tell you it was a good happening.'

'Will you be in Cyprus long enough to have a boat?'

'I'll be here long enough for a lot of things. For instance' . . . he paused . . . 'for living for ever.' He looked directly at Georgia. 'Seriously,' he went on, 'I'll have all the rest of the summer, autumn, and a month or so of winter. I may be over at Rhodes, Crete, but I've wangled it so that Cyprus is my headquarters. Where else would I want?'

She did not answer that, she said, 'And you always loved boats.'

'Just put it down "I loved",' he said.

After that, they did not speak for a long time. They just sat on the cushions that Justin found and let the Mediterranean lap around them, let the soft surge and withdrawal of the sea ease them shoreward, bear them out again. The sun shone down. Georgia slept a little. Before she slipped off, she smiled back at Justin's smiling face.

When she woke he was there beside her, still smiling. She

remembered other smiles that smiling summer . . .

While she still drifted drowsily he made tea in the galley.

'Only hardtack, I'm afraid.' He produced a packet of water biscuits.

'I have a hamper on the beach that Yiannis packed, if you like to row in.'

'Since when have we needed food?' he reproached, and handed her milkless tea and a fistful of biscuits.

She needed nothing else.

They sunned there until the first finger of dusk touched the sky.

'I'd like to take you home, Gigi, but I have to return *Blue Girl*. By the way, I waited this morning, then when you didn't go by, I decided to look the boat over instead.'

'Because it was my day off I didn't take the boys to school, Kate did it,' she explained.

'When is your next day off?'

She told him.

'Will you come out again?'

'Are you going to buy *Blue Girl*?'

'Will you come out again?' he repeated stubbornly.

'Are you?'

'Yes.' He paused. 'That is if you—'

'Yes.' Like Justin, she loved the sea, she could not resist the thought of another sun-soaking, sea-happy day.

'Then I'm buying Georgia,' he smiled. Before she could comment, he said wistfully, 'I wish it was as easy as that.'

She knew what he meant, what he wanted, what he waited for; he needed her to tell him they were going on from where they had left off that summer. She wanted it, too . . . at least she thought she wanted it . . . Justin was as dear to her as ever, and yet—

And yet—

He gave the ghost of a sigh, touched her shoulder briefly, said, 'Next time, perhaps,' then rowed her ashore.

She reached the hill house by dusk. She soaked in a hot bath and was surprised at the sting it gave her – she must have caught the sun.

Kate had fed and put the children to bed, so they sat three at dinner as they always did. Georgia thanked Kate, and the girl said, 'But it's your day off, you're not expected to lullaby two boys, surely.'

'I doubt if they'd let me,' Georgia laughed ... but she was aware that Grip Smith was not laughing.

'You're red,' he said.

'I always am, or so I'm frequently told.'

'*Red*, not any lesser of the roseate hues. Have you been in the sun?'

'Yes.'

'It doesn't seem to have benefited your appetite.' He was looking at her only half-depleted plate; for some reason she was not hungry.

'Yiannis gave me a whacking lunch,' she excused herself.

His brows raised, it gave him a slightly satanic look. 'Which you didn't eat,' he pointed out.

Georgia was wild with herself; how could she have been so stupid as to put the untouched hamper back into the car? Andreas would have carried it to the kitchen, whereupon Yiannis, very touchy about his food, and how it was appreciated, very desirous for everyone to eat up and eat up big, would have raised his hands in distress and sought out the master to report that Miss Georgia must be ill, a *ponus* ... a pain ... perhaps – look, she has eaten nothing of my good lunch.

'Did you eat at a restaurant?' Grip pursued.

'No ... I mean—'

'Did you eat at all?'

'Oh, yes.' Yes, I ate hardtack, Mr. Smith.

'Really, Grip' ... Grip, how quickly Kate had embraced that ... 'you do worry at a bone! Not that you are, Georgia. In fact, you're looking exceptionally fit.'

'She's looking—' But Grip Smith did not finish.

Georgia did not meet Justin at the ramp, but she had not expected to, not now that there was another rendezvous. Rendezvous sounded clandestine, yet there was nothing clandestine there. Justin was free, she was free, she only saw him on a free day. Also, on the morning of the next boating, the sky and the air and the sea were free, beautiful and clear and unsmudged and free. She wore only shorts and bra top, she was going to soak in every bit of the sun that was offered.

As she drew up the little car, she saw that the boat was waiting, that Justin was waiting. He smiled expectantly, and she saw at once why. It was not *Blue Girl* they were going to rim the bays in, but – *Georgia*.

'Justin, you are sweet,' she said.

They set out at once, set out along the beautiful fretted coast, fingers of jutting land, bitten-in bays, pebble stretches, pale pumicy sands. Sometimes they passed barley fields, sometimes olive groves, regimented slopes of carobs, sometimes the old belfries, cupolas, towers and turrets of ancient basilicas.

It was pure delight, and Georgia enjoyed every moment. She had not brought any lunch today, and just as well, for this time there was much more offering than black tea and water biscuits. Justin had literally carried aboard a little feast.

'Fizz, too,' disbelieved Georgia of the champagne.

'Why not? It's an occasion.'

'What occasion?' she asked warily.

'Not the one I think you're thinking . . . unluckily. Well, not yet. At least, Gigi, allow me to say that. Not yet. No, honey, the occasion of *Georgia* instead of *Blue Girl*.' He flicked a few drops of the champagne over the bows. 'That's all you're getting,' he told his boat.

Afterwards he was to sigh that perhaps it was the champagne that did it.

'No, it was just bad luck,' Georgia hastened to reassure him.

'Not bad handling?'

'Justin, you were not to know the sandbank was there.'

'I should have taken the precaution of buying a chart, not just a general coastal map as I have, but a chart.'

'Justin, it wasn't your fault.' She was to add that it could have been worse, that the sand spit could have been rocks, for rocks they did fear they had encountered at first. For suddenly the boat had churned, then stopped, stopped dead.

'Rocks!' Justin had cried.

'There's no tearing sound,' she pointed out.

'It could be right down and the noise drowned. One thing's certain – whatever it is, we're stuck.'

He had dived in, and Georgia had waited anxiously while he examined below to see what was the trouble. He was an expert swimmer, but she was always uneasy when anyone was underneath for a length of time.

She had just been about to dive in herself to look for him when he had come up. He had grimaced as she had helped him aboard *Georgia* again.

'Stuck like a fly on flypaper, absolutely grounded.'

'A sandbank?'

'Yes.'

'Well, one thing, it's not rocks.'

'Dear little Pollyana,' he said unenthusiastically. 'Oh, yes, I'm pleased over that, but not pleased that it's happened at all. It's useless me trying to get her off, I'll need help, and have you noticed lately where the day has gone?'

She looked around, and was startled at the elf light that had crept in while they had been absorbed over their sudden predicament.

'It's almost evening,' she gasped, as indeed it was. In the distance, she did not know where it would be, which town, a necklet of street lights was beginning to sparkle.

'We're here for the night,' he said, 'and though ordinarily I could be jumping for joy for that, what I'm thinking of now is the hue and cry we're going to cause, you with your boss wondering why you haven't returned, me at the wretched hotel that takes such an interest in its guests that every time you don't turn up for a meal they knock on the door. Oh, lord, I ought to be kicked!'

'Justin, it's not your fault.'

'It's so near it doesn't matter.'

'Also,' persisted Georgia, determined to be cheerful, 'we're safe as houses.'

'On a small boat with a sea rising. I'm sorry, Gigi, I shouldn't have said that, but the fact is a sea *is* rising.'

She looked around and saw that the placid blue, now a dark steely blue, was indeed showing unrest. Whitecaps of waves were breaking its serenity. A larger wave veered the boat slightly to one side.

'If it looks really like getting bad, we'll make for shore,' Justin said, 'it's not all that far, and we're both competent swimmers.'

'Yes,' agreed Georgia, but not much liking the idea of that dark, uninviting sea, especially with its rock-strewn beaches, like all the Cyprus beaches, offering only a sharp welcome.

They sat together on the higher side of the boat to try to balance it, to prevent it leaning right over. It was not cold, Cyprus summer nights never were, but there was an edge to the wind that after a few hours of persistence would surely strike chill to the bone.

Justin fortunately had a jacket, but Georgia, thinking she would be home by dusk, had only her shorts and top. Justin took one sleeve of the jacket and Georgia the other, and there they sat as close as one jacket between two people could bring them.

All the shore lights were on now, house lights as well as

street lights. That big cluster of lights they supposed would be distant Limassol.

There was no food left, but anyway neither of them felt like food.

'If this was the old days,' bantered Justin, 'you'd have to marry me. Perhaps it is the old days, perhaps we only think we're up to now. How did that scientist explain it? A long train with its carriages marked Yesterday, Today, Tomorrow. Gigi, let's slip back a few carriages, become yesterday, when you would have had to marry me.'

'Oh, Justin, you are a fool,' she laughed.

'Is that a refusal?' he said in pretended hurt. 'Never mind then, so long as we can advance a few carriages to tomorrow, when you're my wife.'

'I don't know, Justin,' she sighed.

'There's nothing to stop us.'

'That's true, but I still don't know.'

'You're not holding anything against me because of then?'

'No. How could I? It was right what you did. No, I respect you for it.'

'But respect isn't love, is that it?'

'Justin, I don't know. I just don't know. I do know I like you terribly, and I know liking is more important even than loving, but—'

'Before you actually refuse, which you haven't yet, and thank heaven, put your head on my shoulder and sleep on it, the shoulder and the proposal. I don't want you to rush into shoving me off.'

'Off *Georgia*?'

'Could be *Georgia*, too, by the way it's veering now. It may only be a sandbank under us, but I don't want us to be suddenly floundering if the sands happen to move, as is quite likely. If it keeps blowing, honey, we'll just have to swim to shore. But not yet. I'll keep watch. You just relax and build up your strength.'

'Yes, Justin,' she said obediently. It was not the time to be independent, she accepted, it was the time to conform.

She giggled.

'What is it?' he asked.

'I just told myself it was the time to conform, but this is scarcely conforming, is it?'

'You mean convention has finally conquered you and tomorrow we'll put up the banns?'

Her laughter, her 'Oh, Justin' came at the same time as a very large wave. At the same time again as a powerful searchlight, then a long alerting whistle. As the boat keeled over, throwing them both on the sandbank that seemed to be sinking, or moving, very rapidly, the craft behind the searchlight and the source of the alerting whistle loomed darkly into view, not a large boat but powerful and man-oeuvrable. It manoeuvred almost to *Georgia*'s side, and within seconds Georgia herself had been plucked out of the water, Justin after her.

There was a Cypriot at the wheel, a salty, sea-hard fellow as all professional sailors are, but the man who hauled them on to the boat was no seagoer. His hands, as they touched Georgia, if not soft were certainly not hardened. More the hands of someone who worked in an office, she thought abstractedly, at accounts, perhaps, at architecture, at writing. – Writing?

Now she knew why she had flinched instinctively at the feel of those impersonal hands, she knew why, although they were cool, even cold, they had felt hot on her flesh.

They were his hands, Grip Smith's hands. Mr. Smith had come to rescue them. And he had.

Only – shrinking away from the oilskinned figure that in this moment appeared almost to tower over her – being rescued by Agrippa Smith seemed no rescue at all.

CHAPTER EIGHT

APART from throwing her a coat, **Grip Smith** took no notice of Georgia, nor of Justin. He was **too concern**ed with helping the skipper to edge their own **boat away** from the sandbank.

Justin joined in, adding his man strength, and Georgia, shivering in the too large, very rough garment Grip had tossed, wished she could help as well. Anything, she thought, to be occupied and not stand humbled like this. Though why should she feel humbled, she had done nothing wrong or foolish. Justin, either, for that matter, it had been sheer bad luck, not mismanagement, yet he was receiving the same cool treatment as she was. Poor Justin, nothing was going right for him.

But something at last weighed in Justin's favour. The Cypriot said some words to Grip Smith, and evidently Grip understood Greek, though he had never indicated that he had before, for he nodded, then turned to Justin.

'Your boat?' He gave the semi-submerged vessel a mere flick of a glance, but Georgia knew that that flick took in the boat's name. It would, she thought irritably, it just would veer that way, name clearly and unmistakably on top.

'Yes.'

'Not to worry, our skipper says, the bank will cover up no more than it's covered now. It will be a matter for a tug, of course, but you'll get off all right.'

'Thank you, that's a relief. Gigi and I were considering swimming for it, not knowing if the sands would move.'

'Gigi?' Grip Smith asked deliberately, Georgia thought; he would know to whom Justin referred, but he had to humiliate her.

'Georgia – Miss Georgia Paul.'

'Oh, I see.' Again the deliberately unknowing voice. 'As a matter of fact I know Miss Paul. As a matter of fact she is my employee.'

'Oh,' said Justin, taken by surprise. He looked eagerly at Agrippa Smith – the great Agrippa Smith, Georgia knew he was thinking, impressed. Her lip curled at the non-committal way Grip Smith accepted Justin's anxiously outflung hand, his casual pushing aside of Justin's: 'I always wanted to meet you, Mr. Smith,' with a shrugged:

'Well, here I am.' He added, 'And your name?'

'Reynolds.'

'How are you, Mr. Reynolds.'

The boat was clear now, and the skipper was turning it about for its return trip to Limassol. The Cypriot spoke to Grip, and once more Grip addressed Justin.

'Joannides says that if you like he will attend to the tugging off of' . . . a brief pause . . . 'the *Georgia* tomorrow.'

'That would be fine. I expect he's thinking I'm all varieties of a fool not to have taken an itemized chart.'

'I don't think so. In fact I'd be surprised if there was one in existence. Along this stretch of coast there have been six wrecks in the last year, as we were to see while we looked for you.'

'Yes,' came in Justin, 'and you must tell me about that to further dismay me over my stupidity.'

'No stupidity,' insisted Grip Smith, 'as you'll realize after I tell you this story. Money was raised for a lighthouse, Joannides tells me, but, after tenders were called, the villagers voted instead for a church.'

'Putting the responsibility Somewhere Else?'

'Joannides declares devoutly much more efficiently – for, he says, this stretch has no suitable aspect for a lighthouse, but the light from a church lights everywhere.'

'We saw its light tonight,' nodded Justin, 'we couldn't believe the day had deserted us.' He accepted a cigarette from Grip, who gave one to Joannides as well, but took out his pipe for himself. 'How did you come to find us?'

'When Miss Paul did not arrive home after her day's stand-down, we were a little surprised. Though she was not expected officially, she's always very correct in everything she does' . . . Georgia squirmed . . . 'and it was foreign of her not to telephone at least if she was going to be late. I questioned the boys and they were unanimous that she would be either digging worms on a Troodos slope or gathering molluscs on a stretch by the sea.' He laughed shortly. 'They see life, I'm afraid, Mr. Reynolds, only from a bird's eye view.'

'Yes, Gigi has told me.'

'Gigi . . . oh, of course.' Again Gigi squirmed. 'Kate, my secretary, was all for the shops,' Grip went on. 'She insisted that Miss Paul would have run up to Nicosia. We let it go for some hours, then I decided to do some scouting. Luckily the car I obtained for Miss Paul is a good dusk colour—'

'Yellow,' murmured Justin.

'Which made the search easier. I disregarded the worm-seeking, but I did not disregard the beaches. Of late Miss Paul had acquired quite a tan, so I thought the coast would be more likely.

'I was fortunate – I'd barely examined three beaches when I saw the yellow car parked at the northern end of a small bay. I must admit I was a little concerned to find the car and no girl.'

You would have been more concerned, thought Georgia unfairly, to find a girl and no car.

I came back to the hill house and questioned the boys. They were adamant about one thing, and that was that Miss Paul wouldn't drown.' He laughed shortly.

It was encouragement of a sort, I expect, but I'd noticed when I had examined the bay that boats had been ramped there, and it gave me an idea. I contacted Joannides, and he agreed to search for me. He said he had a pretty fair idea where we might find you, and he was right.' Grip looked at his watch. 'All in all it's taken only a few hours,' he congratulated Joannides and himself.

For the rest of the journey back to Limassol, Grip and Justin talked together, and Georgia was surprised . . . and a little piqued . . . at how well they got on. She did not know to what she should put that pique, unless it was feminine frustration that the attention was not on her.

Justin had read Grip Smith's books, and he was a keen critic. He argued a few issues, but lucidly, intelligently, and Georgia, growing more and more incensed, and not helped by not knowing why she should react like this, saw that Grip really enjoyed his company.

When they reached the skipper's jetty, though it was Justin who helped Georgia off the boat, it was Grip who put authoritative fingers under her elbow and led her to his car parked by the harbourside.

'Home for you, Miss Paul, this has been quite an experience. What about you, Reynolds? My hill house? A whisky is called for, surely.'

'It is, but my hotel—'

'I understand perfectly, no doubt an alarm is out already.' Grip put his hand out first this time, and Justin took it. 'See Joannides in the morning regarding your Georgia,' he advised. Then he led Georgia to the car.

They got in silently, he started off without speaking. They went for fully five minutes before Grip broke the quiet. He said: 'Just as well you are sitting down, Miss Paul, and not walking, or you would trip over your bottom lip.'

She sighed audibly. 'I suppose you're waiting for an explanation.'

'Certainly not. Your free day is precisely that. Had you been within informing distance I would have expected a ring, but you weren't, so that's that.'

'So that's that,' she said after him.

'Except . . .'

Ah, she thought, so here it comes.

'Yes, Mr. Smith?'

He turned surprised eyes ... at least he made them surprised, she thought angrily ... on her.

'You were saying?' she prompted.

'You must have misheard. I said nothing. Ah, here we are now, and the good Kate at the door anxious over you. That's a homecoming if you like.'

If I like, thought Georgia — well, I don't like. She felt cross and dishevelled and inadequate. It made it worse that Kate, even in her concern, looked cool, composed and beautiful.

'Dinner has been kept back,' she said.

'Ten minutes, Miss Paul,' Grip Smith advised.

'I don't want any.'

'Of course you want some,' he said irritably.

'Grip' ... how very accustomed Kate sounded to that, how very accustomed Grip sounded now when he said Kate ... 'I believe Georgia knows what she needs. Go and soak in a hot bath, Georgia, then into bed with you, and I'll bring up a tray.'

'What about the boys?' asked Georgia.

'Already in bed, and not over-anxious about you, I must admit,' Kate laughed. 'They both appear to have a deep regard for your efficiency.'

'That's nice, anyway,' Georgia said, and went to her room.

The next few days went by as though nothing at all had happened. Grip Smith questioned her in no way, made no reference to the affair. She should have been satisfied, for liberty to please herself was what she wanted, but she felt he could at least have made some remark about it in passing, have told her how Justin had fared. For she had not seen Justin since that night.

She was anxious about his boat, and every time she returned from depositing the children at the school she glanced in at the ramp. He was never there.

Then on the last morning of the week, Saturday morning, for the Cypriot children attended Saturday school for half a day, she turned the corner and saw a car parked. It was the same colour as Justin's, and that was all she concerned herself with. She had drawn up and got out before she found to her annoyance and embarrassment that it was not the same make of car. It was not Justin who came forward, it was Grip. How could she have forgotten they both had selected a dark-green model?

'So you, too,' said Grip, 'favour the view from here?'

She did not turn round to the blue sea, to the cigar-leaf hills and the damson mountains, she looked to the ground instead.

'You're on your feet now,' he reminded her, 'so you could trip over that bottom lip. You pout a lot, don't you?'

'What is it you want of me, Mr. Smith?'

'I? I thought it was you who wanted, you did the pulling up, you showed the initiative. Or' . . . after a pause . . . 'was it the initiative to see not me but someone else?'

'If you mean—'

'Yes, I do mean, but let's cut it short. I find it a dreary subject, and not worth any stretching out. Why have you been meeting Mr. Reynolds at this spot?'

'It's no—'

'If you're going to say it's no business of mine, skip it, for it is. Anything that happens during your working hours must be my business. Your escapade the other day . . . night . . . was nothing to do with me, it was your stand-down, but when you deviate from your line of duty in working hours I have to be interested.'

'So you're timing me,' she said, 'so long to deliver the boys, so long to return.'

'No,' he drawled.

'Then—'

'Then how do I know you've dallied?'

'Dallied?' The old-fashioned word put her on edge.

'Loitered, then. Simply by watching you from my study window, Miss Paul.'

'You – you snoop!' Her choice of words was childish, and she said it angrily.

'By no means. It's my habit to stand by a window – most authors do, I should say. When I can't compose at a desk I don't sit there chewing my nails, I move around.'

'To the window.'

'Yes,' he said blandly. 'To look out.' As she did not speak, he asked, 'What did you think went on in the office? Two heads never looking up from books?'

'I really couldn't say,' she said coldly. 'I've never been interested enough to wonder, listen, or' . . . deliberately . . . 'look.'

'Well, I looked,' he said, unperturbed, 'and saw your little rendezvous. Mr. Reynolds, I believe?'

'If you saw, there is no need to make a question of it. I encountered him one day, and by chance encountered him several times afterwards.'

'Encountered?'

'That's what I said.'

'There was no design?'

'It's no—' But she stopped herself this time from telling him it was no business of his. 'No fixed design,' she shrugged.

'Why this hill?' he demanded.

'Because' . . . with a sudden resigned rush . . . 'we used to come here.' There, it was out. She had nothing to be ashamed of – why did this man, this hateful Grip Smith make something clandestine of it?

'So, the truth at last! Why didn't you tell me it was the pull of the island that influenced you to accept my employment offer when you did and not the pull of two small boys?'

'Because it was the two small boys who pulled. The – the other was over years ago.'

'For you? For him?'

'For both of us.'

'Yet you both met on a nostalgic hill?'

'Mr. Smith, working hours or not, this is not your business,' she said angrily.

There was a pause, then: 'No. No, it isn't,' he said, and his voice was suddenly subdued. 'I'm sorry, Miss Paul.'

'It's nothing,' she shrugged.

'I did not snoop on you, as you put it, I just looked down and saw a girl and a man on a hill.' He paused. 'As you met once before.'

'Yes. Years ago.' She felt beyond argument now.

'So something happened that you did not reach the usual joyful conclusion of two people on a hill?' He said it so kindly she could not possibly resent it.

'Nothing happened,' she answered dully. 'It simply ended there.'

'And has started again?'

'No. I mean—'

'You mean?'

'I don't know. Please, Mr. Smith, do we have to go on like this?'

'No. But tell me, please, before we close the subject, why didn't you stage that usual joyful conclusion?'

She did not answer.

'Didn't you want the happy ever after-ing?'

'Yes, I did.' It was out before she could stop it. 'But Justin didn't.' She put her hand to her mouth. She was trembling.

'And now?' he persisted.

'Can't I go up to the house, please, do some work, after all this is in working hours.'

Grip moved across and opened the door of the little yellow car for her. He made it clear with a small shrug of his shoulders that he would not probe any more.

'Work well,' he advised, 'for myself, I'll be away until

tonight.'

He bowed as she sparked the engine to life, then ascended again.

Up at the house, Georgia went down to the coop and let the Pink One out for a scratch and a scrape in the ground. It was not because they feared the wading bird would fly off that the Pink One was cooped – that, thought Georgia sadly, was the least of their fears – but because rest was still needed, and that always with an imprisoned bird there was a certain likelihood of harm from a marauder.

The Pink One explored busily, but never once, sighed Georgia, tried those lovely wings. Had he experimented, and failed, so was he frightened to begin again?

She got up, looked cautiously around her, then made a flapping movement with her arms. The Pink One looked away. He *knows*, Georgia felt.

'Well, now I've seen everything.' Kate joined her. 'A human trying to teach a bird to fly! No, Georgia, I'm not laughing. Would you be surprised if I confess I sometimes do it myself? Georgiou and Andreas, too. The boys, of course. Possibly Grip. But I didn't come down for that. You're wanted on the phone, the caller is waiting.' For a brief moment there was a little frown in Kate's lovely violet eyes; she seemed to be trying to reach at something that eluded her.

'Thanks, Kate.' Georgia was on her way.

It was Justin at the other end.

'Hullo there, Gigi, think I'd flown out?'

'I knew you'd have a lot to do, though I've been glancing in at the ramp.' – I got out, too, once, she could have added.

'No need for that,' he assured her, 'not with an official invitation to dinner.'

'Have you?'

'I had it that evening, you couldn't have been attending.'

'Perhaps.'

'I would have availed myself earlier, only *Georgia* has been quite a trouble.'

'Have I?'

'Not you, nor were you ever.' His answer was quick and warm. 'No, Gigi – *Georgia*, boat variety.'

A slight pause, then again from Justin: 'Was it the sec. who answered just now?'

'Yes. Why?'

Another pause, then: 'Nothing. Nothing at all. I want you to ask if I can take up that invitation.'

'Must I?'

'We want to see each other, don't we, and if you're like me pulling in at a ramp isn't quite the way you'd prefer.'

'No,' she sighed.

'Then ask would it be all right some night this week. Look, is Agrippa Smith there now?'

'No.'

'Then not to worry, I'll ask him myself. When will he be back?'

'This evening.'

'Good.'

She inquired rather perfunctorily, 'How is the boat?'

'Your namesake is as perfect as the one it was called after. When are you coming out again?'

Somehow the prospect did not delight her any more. 'We'll discuss it when you come for dinner,' she evaded.

'That will be fine. No, don't worry your little head, don't be bashful, for that's what's really holding you up, isn't it – you don't like asking your big boss for permission to have me there, even though he asked me himself, so I'll do it, Gigi. 'Bye now. Love.' He rang off.

She put the phone down and saw that Kate had returned to the house. The girl gave Georgia a rather long look.

When she collected the boys that afternoon they were full of excitement. It was to be a festival time.

'*Karnivali* . . . *Karnivali!*' they cried, in the Greek manner.

From her last stay in Cyprus, Georgia knew that the carnival period came somewhere around St. Valentine's Day, and she told the children they were months too soon.

'No, no,' they insisted, 'there are many festive days, this is the harvest happiness, there will be lights and clowns and *glikisma* and *siokolata*' . . . they said cake and chocolate with the ease that children do learn the pleasant things before verbs in a foreign language . . . 'all sorts of fun.'

Bish drew a big breath. 'But most of all—'

'The masks,' finished Seg.

'We must buy masks,' they both clamoured, 'then we go from house to house in the masks for money.'

'For the hospital?' asked Georgia.

'No.'

'For animals?'

'No.'

'For poor children?'

'For us,' they explained.

Georgia was horrified, and said so, but the boys, upon arrival at the hill house, ran off and did not listen.

She said she was horrified again at dinner . . . Grip was back by now . . . and told Kate and Grip what the pair intended.

'I won't create,' Grip shrugged.

'For charity, yes, but for themselves!' protested Georgia.

'They spoke about it before to me, and I asked Olympia. Children indeed do wear fancy dress and masks and invade other homes for handouts. It's considered quite all right when the period is carnival.'

'But our children' . . . Georgia flushed, and hated herself for his amused eyes on her pink cheeks . . . '*these* children have more than enough.'

'It might interest you,' Grip drawled, 'to learn that I

haven't given them more than a hundred mil between them for pocket-money per week since I was dumped with them.'

Georgia stiffened at that 'dumped', but she had to see his good sense as regarded their money. She wondered how they had accepted it – they had never complained to her; perhaps like all children the discipline had made them feel secure.

'Then I'm to buy their masks?' she asked.

'Goodness, no! Masking time is a very private affair, it's kept strictly secret. Bish won't even know what Seg has chosen, and vice versa. None of their schoolmates will divulge their choice. Also, once on, the mask is never removed for identification. Even though they choke for breath, they see the secret out. Or so I'm told.'

'Well,' said Georgia, 'it looks as if I'll be driving them to Limassol, then, waiting in the car.'

'No, you'll be in the adult section of the store choosing a mask yourself.'

'I will?'

'Adults recognize carnival as well.'

'You know a lot more of Cyprus than I do.'

'But you were only here one remembered summer,' he said carefully.

'And you?' she asked.

'Not here at all, but I've been years in Greece, in Rhodes, Crete, and more or less the same customs prevail. So look out for a disguise, Miss Paul. You, too, Kate. Your friend of the boat incident' . . . he was looking now at Georgia again . . . 'has rung me up and reminded me that I've invited him to dinner. I feel confident he'll participate as well. Tomorrow night for that dinner. I thought, and we can arrange a night out for the adults as a tribute to carnival. What do you say?'

Georgia said nothing, but Kate was enthusiastic.

'I always wanted to be a—' she began to plan.

'Hush,' Grip reminded her. 'Strictly secret!'

Because he had missed a day's work, he asked Kate to work now, and the two of them retired to the office, where, thought Georgia unkindly, he could not stand at the window at night and *snoop*.

Olympia loved entertaining, and she came to Georgia the next day with a list of dishes from Yiannis they both thought would be nice for the gentleman. Georgia nodded rather listlessly. She wished tonight was over; she was not looking forward to talking to Justin while Grip Smith sat listening to what was said.

After she had put the boys to bed, still excited over the approaching gala, she bathed and dressed, choosing a colour Justin had always liked. When she came out into the passage, it was to see Kate coming down the stairs in the same colour.

'Snap!' Kate called with a laugh.

'I'll change,' offered Georgia.

'No, I will.'

'Neither of you will,' said Grip Smith, joining them. 'That gold suits Kate as well as gold suits you, Miss Paul. I think we'll be having a very rich night.'

He instructed Yiannis about the wine temperatures, then, hearing a car climb the hill, went out to the wide patio.

Justin swung his car to the steps, asked would it be all right there, then got out.

'Gigi, you look a million,' he greeted. 'Good evening, Grip' ... so he, too, was on first names with the great Agrippa Smith ... 'and may I introduce myself to – 'Why – Katherine!' He stood as though turned to stone.

Kate, who had followed the others to the patio, stood incredulous as well.

As Grip Smith said, 'So you two know each other,' Georgia remembered Justin's 'Katherine', Katherine whom he had been engaged to, Katherine because of whom he had not been able to respond when Georgia had said, 'In our home later.'

Katherine . . . Kate. The same girl. The same very lovely, violet-eyed girl.

She stepped aside as Kate stepped forward, as Justin came out of the night to take her extended hand in his.

CHAPTER NINE

BUT that was all there was. Just a handshake. No – 'We've met before.' – 'It's been a long time, Katherine.' – 'How have the years treated you, Justin?' Simply a nod of acknowledgment, and then light talk as Grip led the way to the lounge for pre-dinner drinks.

Here, the conversation flowed easily enough. There was the boat for Justin to account for, how the tugging off had gone, how there had been no more mishaps. Then Mediterranean affairs became the next topic. Was Grip using any of the current happenings in his latest book? As a specialist in world affairs what did he think of the present position? That took them until Olympia came to the door and announced dinner.

The charming arrangement of the table diverted them through the first course. Olympia had availed herself of the present grape harvest, now keeping the pickers and the haulage trucks busy, by forming a horn of plenty as the main decoration. The huge single bunch of large purple grapes extending along the entire length of the festive board was festooned with ribbons, and had been cunningly lit, by Georgiou, with small coloured lights. Resting as it did on the exquisite Lefkara lace cloth, lace learned by the Cypriots from the Venetians many centuries ago, it made a conversation piece that Georgia felt was needed, though, she told herself, glancing at Kate and Justin who were smiling and talking airily enough, we are matured, we are no longer young and green.

It was she who was young, Grip said indulgently, when, in a lapse of the conversation, she called, as the boys had: '*Karnivali! Karnivali! Karnivali* is coming!'

'*Karnivali* is for young and old,' she defended.

He simply raised his brows paternally upon her, and his amicability irritated her much more than his usual astringency could have.

'The boys are masking,' she said. 'They're very excited. It's taken in earnest here. It's a secret affair, not just eye concealment, or some semi-disguise.'

'All the Mediterranean play their games seriously,' came in Grip. 'The adults will dress up, too, and be just as secretive. How about it, Kate and Justin? I thought we might form a foursome and join the port festivities. The Continental is putting on a gay evening. Shall I book?'

They both agreed, if not as gaily, considered Georgia, as the gay occasion seemed to demand.

'It must be secret, though,' warned Grip. 'If we know in advance it would spoil the intrigue.'

'Now who's a child?' Georgia pounced with triumph, but there was never any triumph to be won from Agrippa Smith, he now simply shrugged and made a joke of his seriousness.

The rest of the meal, the remainder of the evening, went smoothly and uneventfully. Even after Justin had departed, Kate said nothing, and apparently felt nothing. She called lightly, 'I'm ready for bed. Good night, both of you.' She went upstairs.

For a few moments longer Grip Smith smoked his pipe. If he had been aware of anything, he made no mention of it, but then unless you had known, as Georgia had known, of a Katherine who undoubtedly was Kate, you would not have noticed any difference in an atmosphere designed strictly to be social and keeping strictly to that plan.

'See to the youngsters that they get what they want for this shindig, Miss Paul,' Grip Smith directed.

'*Karnivali*,' she nodded.

'Fix up your own thing, too. I think' . . . he said the name of the firm at which he had opened an account on her behalf . . . 'should be able to accommodate you.'

'And you?'

'Oh, I'll participate,' he assured her.

'Can I help?'

'It's secret, remember.'

'Yes, but if you need assistance—'

Grip was at the other end of the room, pipe in his mouth. He took it out and laid it down. His eyes were levelled on her.

'Assistance? No. No, it's not assistance I want from you.'

Georgie took it literally. Her cheeks burning, she said 'Good night,' and went to her room. Soon afterwards she heard him mounting the stairs to his room at the end of the hall . . . from Kate's.

It was a long time before Georgia slept.

The next day the school vacation began, though as the boys had so many friends now, Georgia knew a lot of the school activities would continue up in the hill house. Which was good. Although Bish and Seg got on well together, she did not wish them to become the introverted small couple completely dependent on each other that they had been prior to their enrolment in the village school.

Since there was no need to drive them to classes, they begged to be driven instead to the shop on the by-pass where the best masks were. Fortunately it was the store her charge plate covered, so the three of them set out after breakfast in the small car.

As they rimmed the looking-glass sea, peacock blue this morning, Georgia remarked how a pirate's mask, or even one portraying Richard Coeur de Lion who must still haunt these shores, would be in keeping, but, like all the *Karnivali* participants, their little lips were buttoned.

Both boys loved a day in Limassol. They always visited the zoo and aviary, always examined the shops. But one thing they insisted on, and Georgia sighed now as she had hoped the mask-buying would divert them from it, was a soda at the Yellow House in St. Andrew Street, which bore a sign: 'We will answer any query free of charge.'

It had appealed to the pair. Every time they came to town they had a soda and made a query. Georgia was becoming a little embarrassed, though the soda shop lady, like all Cypriot Greeks dedicated almost passionately to the young, did not seem put out, even when Seg had asked her once: 'Were you here, too, when Paul and Barnabas were?'

'No, little one.'

'You're not charging for that, are you, it says so on your sign.'

'No, little one. What is more, you can have this sweetmeat if your mother permits.'

'She's not our mother.'

The proprietress had looked inquiringly at Georgia. The Cypriots had a warm interest in all humanity, but this question was not going to be answered, Georgia had decided, neither freely nor for reward.

She hoped the boys would keep their questions simple today.

They did. They simply asked did the proprietress think it would be fine weather for *Karnivali*?

'But yes. It is always fine weather for *Karnivali*.'

She answered confidently, and Georgia knew she had centuries of foundation to answer like this behind her. For here it was Camelot, and rain, and cold, and snow only came when ordered.

'It will be starry. There will be a big moon,' said the lady.

'You're telling us a lot more than we asked,' said Seg dubiously. 'Will it still be free?'

'Yes, my little ones.' To Georgia: 'Ah, the delights of children!'

Sometimes, Georgia thought.

They drove to the store, and there Georgia was ordered to

remain in the car and watch Seg while Bish chose, then when Bish emerged with his purchase well wrapped she was to watch Bish while Seg chose.

After that they sent Georgia in, checking with each other that neither peeped on her. Laughing at the absurdity of it, but still sufficiently a child herself to enjoy the fun, Georgia went into the shop.

The Cypriots certainly took *Karnivali* seriously, if one could be said to take amusement seriously. The usual goods like wearing apparel, saucepans and pans, had been pushed aside, and now fancy dresses, dresses of all nations, every mask Georgia could have dreamed about, from bird, animal, nursery rhyme, public figure, king, queen, fairy princess, gnome and monster ... many monsters, from benevolent spectacled ones to really gruesome offerings ... hung on every wall, were arranged on every rack, offered themselves on every table.

Georgia felt lost. She did not fancy a bird or animal for herself, though she had no doubt that Grip Smith would have chosen that Bugs Bunny for her, and queens and princesses were also not for her rather unregal type. She did not want a monster, even a kindly bespectacled one. Then she saw Alice, and knew that Alice in Wonderland would be quite all right in any company. She made the purchase and came out again.

The boys looked longingly at her paper parcel, they were childishly consumed with curiosity. Not so Georgia over them, for she could see the shape of a beak in Bish's parcel, and had no doubt he was to be some type of bird at the children's *Karnivali* on the day before the celebration for the adults, and that Seg, judging by that ear peeping out of his purchase, was to emulate Peaceful, the donkey.

But – '*Karnivali, Karnivali!*' that once blasé pair shouted, so nothing mattered, smiled Georgia.

She called '*Karnivali*', too.

As the Yellow House lady had said, *Karnivali* was a fine day. It was the time of the sirocco wind, that kind southerly breeze that blew across from the Sahara, bringing with it a feel of sunsoaked sand, ripe dates, whispering palms. It would be perfect for the festival.

The procession was in the morning, but on the night previous the boys had dressed and masked and joined other dressed and masked confederates ... sheiks, sultans, stone age men, ghosts, robots, monsters in profusion ... jingling their pocket in the hope of mils for *Karnivali* spending. Georgia found, as Grip had found, nothing outrageous in this now, it was simply children's day, and children out to snare as much as they could for the kiddie cars, the hooplas, the spun sugar stall, most of all the stall with the long grape confectionery, which comprised a string that had been lowered into grape syrup time after time until it formed a toffee-hued, sausage-shaped sweetmeat.

It was difficult to pick Bish and Seg; like their friends they never once removed their masks for air. They took it all very gravely. Georgia put the bird down as Bish, the donkey head as Seg, but knowing that crafty pair, quite likely they were fooling her, and masking the other way about. Just to make sure of confusion they could have changed with any of the boys. Voices could not help, either, not emerging as they did from papier maché.

In the end, Kate, Grip and Georgia stopped trying to crack the mystery, and handed over coins instead, small value coins to a pair who only a month ago had calmly signalled and taken a taxi, who had probably, drawled Grip, lit their chocolate cigars with a banknote.

The children got into the procession, and Grip drove the girls to a hotel whose verandah had been offered to him.

It was an exciting parade. The skirl of the bagpipes of a visiting Scottish regiment led it, then an army band helped out, local bands, groups of singers and serenaders. The floats were ambitious, the clowns on stilts hilarious. *Karnivali*,

Karnivali – it was everywhere. Everyone clapped and was glad. Balloons soared, streamers were flung.

'You have pink snow on your hair,' Grip said to Georgia as they pushed through the crowds to the car again. 'Can't you ever get away from that colour?'

She put up her hand to remove the confetti.

'No,' he said abruptly, 'don't.'

She looked at him, surprised.

'*Karnivali*,' he said.

The boys were put to bed before tea that night, a tray taken to them. They were absolutely exhausted.

'Did you guess who we were?' they giggled at Georgia as she sat at the end of the bed.

'Yes, I think both of you changed with Mathos and Christophus to fool me, I think you were the sheik that everyone thought was Mathos, Bish, and you were the monster everyone thought was Christophus, Seg.'

They laughed triumphantly. 'We knew you would,' they said shrewdly, 'so we were just what we brought, a bird and a donkey.'

'Tomorrow,' said Seg, 'we're going to dress up for Buttons, Purr, Peaceful and the Pink One. Do you think they'll know we're humans?'

'We'll see,' said Georgia. 'Tomorrow I dress up, too.'

'Don't tell us, let us guess.'

'Yes, darlings, but it's been a long day. Sleep now.'

She need not have directed it, the boys had already slipped off.

There were more masked visits the next day. As Grip said feelingly of an emptied pocket, empty of jingle: 'The young never know where to stop.'

Georgia, who had had a hilarious morning with the boys as they had tried to fool the menagerie, and was in *Karnivali* mood herself, retorted: 'Tonight we won't know where to stop.'

'What *do* you mean, Miss Paul?' he said in mock scandal, and, as ever, her flags of embarrassment had shown in her cheeks. He had laughed as she had gone off.

They were to dine in the Continental at eight, but to keep up the secret spirit of the frolic there were to be no pre-drinks, no pre-conversation. The big car would be drawn up at the steps, and the girls were to get in and be driven to the hotel. The men were going separately and would meet them at the reserved table.

By half past seven, Georgia was ready, and she ran to the boys' room to let them see her.

She was a little deflated at their silence. Either they did not like her get-up, or could not recognize it, yet it was still attractive, and they were pretty knowledgeable small fry.

She stood waiting . . . and waiting . . . Then:

'We don't know who you are,' said Bish.

'You're Alice in Wonderland,' said Seg, 'but which?'

Somewhere in the house, a clock chimed, and becoming Cinderella instead of Alice, Georgia ran out, leaving the boys to their wonder, even though it made her wonder. Then she stopped wondering. Coming down the stairs was another Alice, which made for sense, for all the masks, though varied in type, were similar. Kate, too, had chosen to be Alice.

'Snap!' called Kate, as she had before.

'What do we do?' laughed Georgia.

'Too late to do anything, and anyway, it should make for fun.'

Giggling, they went out to the car.

It was a magic night. The Cypriots, always akin to nature, to the time and the tune of the year, had selected full moon, a great gold cut-out of a moon. The stars were magnificent.

The streets teemed with people. It was as though every adult had watched the children at play and resolved that it was their turn tomorrow. It took a long time for Georgiou to get the car to the Continental's canopied front.

The girls got out, received a cannonade of confetti as they ran up the red carpet, then into the hotel.

From that moment, it was a mad, mad whirl.

A table had been booked, but Georgia only saw it once in the entire evening. As soon as she entered the candlelit interior, she was seized upon by revellers, the other Alice the same, and from then on it went a merry way.

In the short period when she did visit their reservation it was to discover with amusement that the same as had happened to Kate and herself had happened to the men. For the girls had two sheiks as escorts. It was not surprising, really, Georgia thought, for when it came to male masks, if one was not a comedian, or monster addicted, there was not so much choice.

She had no chance to think about that, though, she was grabbed by a pirate and whirled away in a waltz.

Whirled then by a cutting-in space man to perform a rhumba, by a king to do a tango, after that all the foot-tapping dance tunes the two alternating bands supplied.

Then a third band was rendering bouzouki music, and Cypriots . . . men only as was the tradition . . . were taking the floor in Zorba style. They danced seriously, even gravely, very emotionally, and Georgia felt her senses accelerating with the accelerating rhythm.

She had seen it before, and had swayed then, as now, to the intoxication of it, to the strange experience, for experience was all she could call it, of arm-entwined men moving as if impelled not by themselves but by some other source backwards and forwards to the haunting notes. That they wore odd clothes now only added to her deep impression, and she was not aware until a hand drew her to her feet and led her to the dance floor again that the bouzouki theme had ended, that a waltz again was drifting round the room.

She danced in the sheik's arms a little drunkenly, drunk from the gipsy strains of the bouzouki . . . a little drunk, she thought, too, from the sweet Aphrodite wine that had been pressed on her.

The sheik . . . was he Justin, Mr. Smith or one of the several sheiks present? . . . danced as well as anyone could in such a crowd. She looked up, trying to see the eyes through the mask, but it was only half light, streamers were being flung, and the disguise was a concealing one.

She could feel cool fingers, though, cool fingers that still somehow gave a warm sensation to her flesh. Was it— Or was it—

The lights went out for a moment. In the brief silence that the shock of complete darkness imposed on all the revellers, a voice said softly from behind the mask, so softly no one else would hear . . . yet Georgia heard:

'Dear, dear Kate.'

They were back in the hill house again. Justin had come for a final nightcap. He and the girls sat on the patio while Grip went in for the drinks, since it was now early morning, and the staff long in bed.

They laughed over the night's festivities, over the remarkable coincidence of both parties, male and female, choosing the same masked disguise.

'I always fancied myself as a sheik,' Justin said. He had discarded his mask and headdress, loosened his voluminous robes. 'How do they stand it in that heat?' he marvelled. 'It's good to be a westerner again.'

'Not so good to be out of Wonderland,' proffered Kate. 'I quite enjoyed my picture-book world tonight.'

'Yes, I saw you were having a ball.' There was a dry note in Justin's voice. He gave Kate such a quick glance, it was barely even a flick.

'Perhaps you were seeing Georgia,' Kate suggested blandly.

Any rejoinder Justin might have made was prevented by Grip wheeling out sandwiches as well as drinks.

'I had a feeling,' he explained of their cries of appreciation, 'that the night would be so hectic there would be little time for sustenance, so I had Yiannis cut up some in readiness.' He, too, had removed his mask and headdress, loosened the robe.

'Help yourself, Alice One,' he said to Kate. 'You too, Alice Two,' to Georgia.

'When the boys were nonplussed tonight I thought I'd chosen badly,' Georgia said, munching her sandwich.

'They'd seen me previously,' Kate laughed. 'What an instance of great minds thinking alike!'

'Yes,' Georgia agreed, putting aside a question that she had known ever since that last waltz and Justin mistaking her for Kate that she must ask herself. Ask herself how she had felt, how she felt now, about Justin, Justin whom she had remembered ever since that remembered summer, Justin who had comprised every summer ever since for her, Justin for whose memory she really had come back to Cyprus, Justin who was her first love . . . and still her only love? . . . whispering:

'Dear, dear Kate.'

She did not feel hurt, she found . . . not yet . . . Perhaps it would come, perhaps she was just numb now, not up to the stage of realizing that Justin, who had climbed a hill in her memory, run to her when he had found her on that hill, could turn to Kate . . . Katherine to him . . . and, forgetting One Summer, say: 'Dear, dear Kate.'

She tried to feel something definite, something either to tell her that she was unhappy, something to tell her instead she was untouched. But it was no use, there seemed nothing indicative.

Their voices drifted around her, the usual after-party voices, wanting to seek sleep but too sleepy and relaxed to move.

Then sharply, imperatively, a consciousness was pushing, no, *nudging* at Georgia. Justin was taking up his Arab headdress, playing with the braid, trailing it through his fingers.

She glanced at the headdress that Grip had thrown down.

Identical. Identical in every way ... except colour. Justin's was blue, Grip's red.

Though the Continental had been in semi-light, though cigarette smoke and streamers had made it even more obscure, one fact was definite in Georgia's mind; it was almost as though she had colour-photographed the scene. That scene in which one sheik wore a blue band, one sheik a red.

It had been a red band when the voice had whispered mistakenly: 'Dear, dear Kate.'

Red stood for Agrippa Smith.

Georgia leaned back, closed her eyes. She wished that closing them could cut out that headband, but the darkness she imposed upon herself seemed to make the colour stand out more than ever.

Grip Smith, not Justin. Grip saying quietly: 'Dear, dear Kate.'

Grip saying it.

'No!'

She was not aware she had exclaimed aloud until she opened her eyes and saw the three of them looking at her.

'I must have dozed off,' she excused herself.

'And had a nightmare during the doze, by the sound of you. Who were you refusing, Miss Paul?'

That 'Miss Paul', said her fuddled senses, made it Grip Smith speaking to her, of course.

'What do you mean?' she asked.

'You said very forcibly "No!"'

'Did I?' She gave a careless shrug, never feeling less careless in her life. Yet it was not Grip saying that to Kate that was gripping her, it was – her own reaction now. She could not believe it. A reaction to Justin saying it, yes, but not, and never, to Grip Smith.

'I must be ready for bed if you tell me I was talking in my sleep,' she said, and rose.

Grip rose, too.

Kate seemed inclined to linger a while, then she got up. Justin murmured something to Grip, blew a kiss to both the girls, then went to his car.

Georgia afterwards could not remember bidding the upstairs good night, she only remembered going to her room and sitting emptily down on the bed.

Above her she heard their footsteps . . . Kate's, Grip's.

But in her mind she was not hearing footsteps but a voice.

'Dear, dear Kate,' the voice said.

CHAPTER TEN

IT was the intensity of the protest in her that shook Georgia.
That shocked her. Agrippa Smith not only is nothing to me,
she told herself, but I actually dislike him. Why, oh why, am
I reacting like this to words said to me while thinking I'm a
different girl? It's Justin who matters to me, and always has,
and even if the years have changed me from eighteen,
changed my outlook, though I'm still not sure about that and
I can't say truly, then I *am* sure and I *can* say truly one
thing: I don't care for Agrippa Smith.

He's everything I shrink from, hard, astringent, unbend-
ing. So why am I unsettled like this?

Anyway, assuming I did *not* dislike him, what future
could there be? A man who never leaves his office for hours,
hours with a girl like Kate? A man so carried away with that
girl he even speaks her name to someone else without first
ascertaining that he's indeed talking to Kate? As he was
not.

Where is my pride? she asked herself a dozen stupefied
times, and received the same stock answer. There is no pride
in love. She had read that in books many times. But good
heavens, she felt like crying, I don't love, I could never love,
that autocrat.

She mulled it over, she began at the beginning again and
mulled over it a second time. And got no further.

Summer was waning. The last of the grape trucks were
labouring over the slippery, juice-strewn roads with their
purple loads. The hammering heat was a forgotten thing.
The thyme and rosemary were withering to brown clumps.
The scilla, that had looked as though it had been washed in
sky, was a gaunt wreck. Winter pumice, drab and ochre, were

149

taking over all the flamboyant colour; the pine trees had already spread carpets of needles; the Mediterranean was staging a backdrop change from celestial to iron-blue, often with white-capped waves that sifted the shingle on the beaches with an angry little hiss.

Yet never, thought Georgia, looking at the bare branches of the fruit trees around the hill house, had Cyprus been more beautiful. She had thought that summer brought everything to this island, but now shape and contour emerged unblurred, unadorned by leaf and flower, and it was almost achingly lovely.

The shops were getting ready for Christmas, the same Yuletide adornment as in the west except that here Santa Claus gave way to a benevolent picture of some revered, long departed old priest. The kindly holy man was imposed everywhere – on the silver wrappers of chocolates, on trinkets to decorate a room. He smiled down from shop awnings and even twinkled in electric light arches above the streets. His message, Georgia told the boys, was Peace, just as that was the message everywhere.

Up in the Troodos Mountains, Mount Olympus was putting out the island's first tablecloth of snow. Later in the season the cloth would reach right down, hang pretend white flowers on all the trees, other mountains would copy loftier Olympus, but just now only the highest peak wore a snowy crown.

Georgia took the boys up one day, passing through Platres with some of its trees still clinging to their autumnal red and gold, unwilling to lose their loveliness even for a few months, which was all their winter would last. On an island where seasons touched hands there were no sharp divisions, Georgia found.

But once on Olympus, autumn was finished, the snow was on the ground, thin, a trifle bedraggled, but snow.

The boys enthused over it. They had been to St. Moritz, Kitzbühel, other expensive, exclusive slopes, but this was *their* snow. They made inadequate balls of it and laughed happily. They laughed because they were happy, Georgia knew.

'Do you like Christmas?' she asked them.

They could give her no decided opinion.

'Have you ever had a Christmas tree?' she asked then.

Oh, yes, they had had that, their mother always had fine trees installed, trees with lights and spotlights and floodlights and—

'Your own tree,' Georgia came in. 'Your own special tree you put in a tub yourself, that you decorated yourself with cones you gathered yourself, and painted yourself?'

They were looking at her eagerly, wistfully.

'Could we?'

'Of course. We'll gather cones now.' There were plenty of cones dropped from the trees. 'Also,' went on Georgia, 'we'll make our own presents.'

'*Make* them?' they echoed.

'From all sorts of things. This piece of wood, for instance, I know Kate would love. You could paint and fix it in a frame for her. Like this.' She showed them.

'Now, Mr. Smith. He does a lot of writing. A paperweight would be grand. I saw some marvellous lucky stones down in the brook running from the tiny tarn. You could choose a good smooth stone and polish it with some stuff I know.

'Then Olympia—' she went on.

'And Yiannis and Georgiou and Andreas,' said Bish.

'And Peaceful, Buttons, Purr and the Pink One,' said Seg.

'You, Georgie,' they both said together.

'And you,' nodded Georgia back.

They started exploring, and collecting. Things for a tree. Things for gifts. There was no fear of them becoming lost, the scene was winter-bare, no secretive leaves or boughs to hide small busy figures, and the snow still had not attained any concealment properties.

Not then . . .

Georgia did not know at what period she realized it was snowing, *really* snowing. All the time there had been a small drift, more a mizzle than a fall, so she supposed that that was why she had not noticed till now. As for the boys, they had forgotten snow in the enthusiasm of outdoing each other in decorations and gifts. Their heads were down . . . one head by the rune, one under a tree fast becoming powdered in soft white. It was the tree that caught Georgia's attention first. She gasped in surprise, then looked around.

She was amazed at how much snow had fallen, all the criss-cross marks on the thinner snow had been ironed out. The verges at the sides of the road were thick white banks. The road itself . . .

Oh, no! she cried silently in dismay. Where before the mountain road had been a reassuring dark blue bitumen track, now it was no track at all. There was only white. More and more white.

She did not call the boys at once, she went quietly through a thicket of trees . . . a white thicket . . . her feet sinking deeper with each step until she could see the car parked by the side of the bitumen, or what once was the bitumen. Now it was just a continuance of snow.

She went to the car and examined it. She looked at where the road should be. Even if she could get the car on to it she could see that she could not travel along it any more, not without the aid of chains.

She knew that the snow-plough only operated at weekends, and that then its activities were restricted to periods when tourists were expected. It was too early in the season for tourists – besides, pre-Christmas was always a slack time for any resort.

Georgia leaned against the car and tried to think. It was still bright, but the dark up here would come early, and with it an intense cold. They could not stay in the car. They could freeze. The only thing to do was to start down now on foot while they could still pick a way, find some car, or so Georgia hoped, in the lower regions that could give them a lift to town. Or anyway, somewhere *safe*. She thought with distaste of Grip Smith's raised brows, of the things he would find to say, but she made the thoughts brief. She had two children to get to safety and that must be her sole concern.

The boys, when told as casually as she was able, were supremely unafraid and very reluctant to leave. They had collected a pile of goodies that they declared the snow would hide if they didn't hide them themselves in the car. Georgia squandered precious time helping them carry the cones, stones and branches across to the boot, a boot already well blanketed in snow, but in their collecting obsession the boys did not notice.

At last they agreed to start down the mountain, making fun of the fact that the road was barely discernible, only two banks of piled snow with a flatter surface between them suggesting it was indeed there. Thankful for their cheerful co-operation, unintended though it was, Georgia pretended to join in the fun.

But each step she took she felt less happy, and when the steps began to get quite deep, much deeper than steps on a road should get, she felt certain they had detoured from the bitumen, or what beneath the snow should be bitumen. But the children loved it. Seg went into gales of mirth when Bish trod into a drift up to his knees, whereupon Bish retaliated with a snowball, and it was on.

To give herself time to think, for by now she was really alarmed, Georgia joined in the throwing. Then she suggested making a snowman, and while the boys were occupied she ran through the trees to look around. She could see nothing at all but snow.

She came back again, slowly, fearfully. As an Australian she knew little of snow. What was the best to do? she wondered. Return to the car?

And where was the car?

Keep cool ... keep cool ... She could have laughed at that had not nervous tears filled her eyes. If they rolled down, she thought ridiculously, they would freeze. Yet that was foolish, actually it was not cold yet, not with the snow falling. The cold would come later ... and where would they be?

She came back to the snowman. Because there was ample material he was quite a substantial man. Bish had put in a stick pipe, which was suitable, for this man's name, she read, was Grip.

'You shouldn't write Grip,' she reproved mechanically.

'We know, but we never bother with that other.'

No, she had never heard them say Father ... Dad ... Pop ... any of the paternal tags. But why was she wasting time like this? She didn't want to panic, or at least let them sense her panic, but she had to make a move, and soon. But where?

Then she heard Seg saying casually: 'Look, the snow-plough is coming up and there's a car behind it, a car with chains. Why, it's his! It's Grip's! Best not to let him see what we did, Bish.' They began tumbling down the snow-man.

But Georgia was tumbling down the slope to the approaching car, not caring whether the tears on her cheeks froze or not.

Grip had pulled the car up when he saw her, and had got out. He caught her as she slid down the last bank, caught and held her against the rough wind-breaker he wore.

'Oh, Grip, Grip!' she called.

'Steady, young 'un,' he came back.

'Grip, I'm so sorry, I didn't mean to do this, I was a fool, we could have frozen, the boys could have—'

'Steady, I said. And what is all this? All I can see is a sudden snowfall and a stranded car.'

'But – but stranded where?' she sobbed. 'We could have

been out all night. We would have died.'

'With a hotel round the next bend?' he scoffed. 'With a string of houses? Oh, yes, there is a string of them. With some shops.'

She looked at him incredulously. 'Is there?'

'Yes,' he assured her.

She tried to mumble apologies for her stupidity; she deserved, she said, everything he said to her.

'Look,' he answered, 'you've done nothing, you little idiot. You didn't know the weather was going to play up, even the weather men didn't know, it was completely unpredicted. Especially for this initial period of the winter season. When I heard the news on the radio I guessed you'd be caught, so I got out the car, took the precaution of adding chains, took the precaution when I arrived at Platres of persuading the snow-plough to do a circuit, and here we are, all safe and sound.'

'No thanks to me,' she sniffed.

'My, we are wearing sackcloth and ashes today, aren't we?' He gave her a grin. 'Hi, kids!' he called as she could only raise a trembling smile in return. He tactfully turned his back.

He reversed his car ready to descend again, put them in it, then went up on the snow-plough to check Georgia's car. In a few minutes he was back again . . . they must have taken a circular track from the little yellow model, for Georgia felt sure they had trudged much longer than that. Trudged *hours*.

Driving carefully over the slippery road, they came down the mountain again. But not right down. Just below the snow-line, or at least where what snow did fall was confetti thin, merely a powdering of white, Grip pulled up at a small inn.

'Hot chocolate called for,' he said.

The boys whooped in, but Georgia, though just as anxious for hot chocolate, moved much more soberly.

'I have to advise it once again,' Grip grinned. 'Don't trip over that bottom lip.'

They sat by a blazing fire and drank the chocolate. Then the proprietor came in very excited to tell them that this was the first time, the first, sir and madam, that snow had fallen this low. A sprinkling, yes, but not snow as was falling now. He had been here, he said, for many years, but never seen it like this.

They stood at the window with him and watched it, and what more lovely a sight, more comforting a sight, than snow from behind glass and in a firelit room.

'It's beautiful,' Georgia said impulsively, all her fears gone now.

'That's better,' Grip smiled.

He left them a while. 'Perhaps,' said Bish hopefully, 'it's for more chocolate.'

But it was to be for toasted sandwiches as well, a large honey cake. A bottle of wine for the adults as well as more chocolate for the boys.

'Sorry,' said Grip Smith, 'that I can't rustle up a more formal meal, but actually the hotel isn't really functioning yet, it hasn't started its seasonal swing, that doesn't come until the late January Mount Olympus falls. This one today, as you heard, was a freak.'

'But do we have to stop for a meal?' Georgia asked.

'You just said it was beautiful, isn't that reason enough?'

'Reason, but not compulsion. Besides, it will be after bedtime for the boys when we get back.'

'We're not going back,' he said calmly. 'We're all staying here for the night.'

'But—'

'Look, you've had quite an afternoon . . . and so have I.'

'I'm sorry,' she said again.

'Not that,' he came in impatiently. 'A tricky part of my MS. It was refreshing to get away from it for a while, but frankly I've had all the refreshment I want, and now I'm plain, ordinary tired. It's not the easiest of drives, as you know yourself, not with all those curves. I've rung up Kate, so there'll be no hue and cry, and mine host is attending our rooms. *Now*,' he said next with a resigned sigh, 'you're going to murmur "Pyjamas" . . . "Toothbrushes" . . .'

'I wasn't.' She was not aware she said it eagerly until she heard her own voice.

He grinned at her. Georgia smiled back. They turned together and told the boys, who applauded the idea.

The hot sandwiches disappeared, and more were brought. By the time more chocolate had been consumed, the wine depleted, Georgia said if their room was ready she would put the boys to bed.

The proprietor apologized that his good wife was not here yet to do the domestic side of the inn – Madam must understand that the skiers did not come until after Christmas, but he had prepared accommodation upstairs himself.

She prised the boys from the window, telling them they could watch the snow even better up higher, and they followed her as she followed Mr. Christodoulou up the winding flight to a charming raftered room, where she soon had Bish and Seg in bed, too warm, too comfortable, too sleepy to hanker after more snow. She waited only a few moments for them to slip off, then came downstairs again, to the fire, to the snow beyond the window, to Mr. Christodoulou plying perhaps the island's most popular drink, brandy sour, but made on this occasion more in the form of *glüwein*, since it was winter, and a man's stomach needed heat. Mr. Christodoulou had a comfortable big stomach, which he patted as he said this.

They sat well into the night, talking of island affairs, of island wisdoms and lore.

Then mine host rose, apologized for keeping Sir and Madam, and trudged off to bed in an adjoining house. 'For,' he informed them shrewdly, 'when the season is on it is a good thing not to be under the same roof.'

For some time still Georgia and Grip sat on, sat opposite sides of the fire, staring at the fire. Dreaming their own particular dreams, for fires are like that.

Then somewhere a clock chimed, and Georgia, too, got up. Grip rose after her. Together they climbed the stairs.

Then there was a predicament. Although there was a string of rooms, only one room, beside the boys', had been prepared. Grip opened door after door, cancelled darkness only to reveal bare beds.

'He must have thought we—' he said.

'Didn't you tell him?' she asked.

'I said Madam and two boys. I naturally thought—'

'He naturally didn't think,' she snapped.

Grip said: 'Or he naturally thought . . .'

It looked as though a mild quarrel was going to emerge, and after what she had gone through, that was just too silly.

'You could rouse him, rouse Mr. Christodoulou,' Georgia suggested.

'Go next door. Go out of this warm inn, bring him back again, send him home once more.'

'It does seem unfair,' she agreed.

'It's totally unfair.'

She nodded. 'But what else?'

He did not answer . . . and into that non-answering crept something so close, so warm – so sweet, that Georgia had to turn away.

Going into her room . . . their room, the proprietor had thought . . . she gathered up a pile of blankets, for there were many more than she could possibly need. Coming back to him, she said a little indistinctly: 'Here you are.'

Grip just stood there.

Now she said hurriedly: 'Would you like me to make up one of the beds?'

He still stood.

Again, somewhere, a clock chimed. It broke something, not a spell, but – something. He took the blankets. He said: 'No, no need. I'll doss downstairs. Keep the fire going.' He looked at her another long minute, then he went.

But Georgia stood on for longer again. She stood on so long in fact that a quarter hour chimed. Then she turned and went to bed.

She was awakened the next morning by the sound of laughter under her window. She ran to look out of the window to see the boys throwing snowballs at each other.

Because they were only barely on the snow line here, the snow had already melted, and the leftovers they were pelting were more ice than snow.

'You'll catch cold!' Georgia called down.

She dressed hurriedly, brought the boys in for a hot breakfast mine host had cooked, then still worrying about their wet clothes, for the snow fight had been a thorough one, they all bundled into the car, Grip telling her not to be concerned about her own car, he would have Georgiou see to that, then made their way home to Amathus.

As she had feared, before they got there the first sneezes set in. They were certainly marked, Georgia could see, for 'flu.

Upon arrival she had Grip ring for the doctor.

'For a sniff!' he demeaned.

'They were soaked,' she protested.

'Of all the fusspots!'

'Please, Mr. Smith,' she appealed, 'otherwise I will feel responsible.'

Doctor Papademetriou came and said yes, certainly chills, but only common chills, not even calling for any mild medicine. Just put the boys to bed and allow them citron and *meli*.

'Hurrah, honey!' they called. They loved honey.

They were to stay in bed for several days, since there was a slight . . . slight only . . . temperature, the doctor said.

Georgia got out Pirates' Den, then, on an inspiration, she started them on their Christmas gifts and tree decorations. They loved this so much it seemed in the end they would have to be prised from their beds and their preoccupations, that only the Pink One would ever achieve results.

'Those children are too angelic,' Grip said once.

'They're busy,' Georgia nodded.

'Good for you. What is it? Pirates' Den?'

'No, Peace on Earth, Goodwill to Men.'

'Is that a game?'

'It's life. It's Christmas.' Because she loved Christmas, because she and John had been a Christmas kind of family, Georgia said: 'Christmas is miracles-made and dreams-come-true, didn't you know?'

'Yes, I knew,' he said slowly, looking at her, 'but—'

Something in that 'but' told her that this was not going to be the usual objection that you could argue back against, possibly break down, and she waited.

'But the children will be home for Christmas,' he said.

'Of course.'

'I said home, Miss Paul.' He let the emphasis sink in. 'Of course,' she said again, but this time a little uncertainly, faintly sensing doom.

'Home,' he told her a third time.

'—is where the heart is.' She spoke unthinkingly, and the next time he came in it was quite harshly with:

'No, home is where you are obliged to go, that is when you are aged six and seven. Home in this instance is . . . let me see, where will this Christmas be held? Ah, here we are.' He had opened a small notebook. 'Salzburg. Sigrid is having Christmas at Salzburg.'

'With—' Georgia said, bitterly disappointed.

'With her sons.' His lips were thinned. She noticed that even in her disappointment. She also noted that he would not put himself in the picture and say 'our sons'.

Now there was a long pause.

'So they're going up to Salzburg for Christmas,' Georgia murmured, deflated.

'Yes.'

'I see.' She went to the window to stare out up at the Troodos, at the white tablecloth a little lower on the mountain table. She felt very empty.

She thought of Christmas here without the children and didn't like the thought. Christmas needed children . . . or at least it needed something more than Grip Smith had to offer – to offer her, anyway. With Kate it would be different. 'Dear, dear Kate,' she recalled.

'How long will they be away?' she asked.

'Only for the accepted festive period, that will be enough for Sigrid.'

'Then I'll go away, too – I mean, there's no need to pay me while there's nothing for me to do.'

'You're going away, anyway,' he said coolly, 'for which you will be duly paid. You are to accompany the children to Salzburg.'

'There's no need, air hostesses are very sympathetic, most reliable.'

'You're not attending, Miss Paul – *you* are taking the boys to spend Christmas with their maternal parent.'

'Not their paternal one?' she asked.

A hard look came over his face. 'No,' he said shortly, 'not the paternal one. Not now. Not ever.'

'I don't know the boys' mother.' She did not say 'your wife' because he never did, because for all she knew it was ex-wife, estranged wife.

'Nor will you, probably. Anyway' . . . a long look at her, at the pinkness of her . . . 'you would be one of the last that Sigrid would care to know.'

'What do you mean?'

'Oh, skip it,' he said irritably. 'I'm just telling you that Sigrid wants her offspring around her at Christmas and I want you to fly up with them, deliver them. Easy enough, surely.'

'Yes, but where—'

'Where will you be? I thought of Munich with your own folk. There' ... a little laugh ... 'that at least raises a smile.'

'Oh, yes,' said Georgia, for it did. To be with John for Christmas! With Leone! The imps! The happiness of family. It made the loss of the tree nothing, it made—

'Well, I've made *you* contented, anyhow,' Grip Smith said abruptly, so abruptly she looked quickly at him. He did not seem happy, she thought. She wondered if Kate had said that she, too, would be away.

'If you'd sooner—' she fumbled.

'Sooner what?'

'Nothing, I mean—'

'I have the tickets ready,' he said matter-of-factly, 'I'll leave it to you to tell the boys.'

The boys had painted two boxes of cones, made stencils of reindeer, strung silver bottle tops together for bells, moulded plasticine Christmas trees and tinted them.

They were not pleased.

'Our mother,' they said bleakly in unison.

'Boys!' Georgia reproved.

'Christmas up there,' they moaned.

'I'm going up, too,' she told them.

They brightened a little. 'Will you be with us?'

'No, with my own family. But I'll come back with you.'

Back. At least Georgia saw they had that to hold on to. And hold on they did.

'When we come back—' they said.

'After we're back—'

'I think we'll bring back with us—'

Back, back, back.

Kate was going to England for the season. Justin would have been in Rhodes, anyway, on business.

'What about you, Mr. Smith?' Georgia asked.

'I'll enjoy some peace and quiet,' he said, 'for a change—'

She looked at him, but could not have said whether or not he meant that.

On Christmas Eve, muffled up in sweaters and scarves, in gloves and warm boots, feeling over-clad in the less-than-cold of Nicosia's mild December – mild, anyway, compared to Europe's Christmas – Grip drove them to the airport and saw them off. Kate had already gone. Justin had left last week.

The great plane came in and they were driven by bus across the field. Georgia took out Pirates' Den to amuse the boys during the flight, but they were not inclined for it. Something seemed to have settled on them. They were bored, listless, they were blasé again.

'The service isn't good,' complained Bish.

'I've been in better lines than this,' demeaned Seg.

It was bitterly cold when they landed at Salzburg. Inside the plane they had been warm, insulated, now the chill fairly cut at them. Georgia had forgotten in Cyprus how very cold cold can be.

She went through Customs, then emerged with the boys.

'That will be us,' said Bish gloomily of a uniformed chauffeur waiting in the reception hall.

'How do you know?' asked Georgia.

'It's always us when it's like that.'

She gathered he meant looking like that, and asked no more.

The man came up, showed his credentials, and Georgia followed the boys to a large, expensive car that awaited.

'Good-bye, Georgie,' they called, 'see you in a week.'

'Just a week, darlings,' she assured them, and had the satisfaction of seeing them actually smile.

'Just a week,' they clung.

Georgia took a train for her final lap to Munich.

She certainly enjoyed herself on her Christmas break. It

was some years since she had had a family festival, and Leone had done all the things Georgia had wanted to do for Bish and Seg. There was everything to make Christmas, most of all the human ingredients. The only times that Georgia felt an inadequacy was when she thought of Bish and Seg, who had patiently painted all those cones for nothing. Everything for nothing, they must be thinking. She did not let herself think of Grip Smith spending a Christmas alone. Anyway, he had his peace and quiet.

Munich was so convenient to snowfields that all the snow pleasures that Troodos had to wait for nature to bestow thickly were satisfactorily and sufficiently here for the taking without any waiting. The days were full of tobogganing, skiing, snowballs, snowmen; at night there was singing, playing charades, toasting marshmallows by a crackling fire.

'One day more, old girl,' John said one morning.

'Yes.'

'Don't go, Aunt Georgia, stay with us,' the imps begged.

'I have work to do,' she told them, 'duty calls.'

'Does anything else call?' asked Leone pertly. 'Anyone?'

'Don't answer that,' advised John. 'My wife is an incorrigible snooper.'

'Two little boys call,' Georgia informed her sister-in-law. 'Will that do you?'

'If you say so,' regretted Leone, disappointed.

The family drove Georgia to the Salzburg terminal, making a day of it, then, having deposited her there warm and secure, decided, since the weather was unpleasant, even threatening, to make for Munich and home again. She stood at a long glass window waving to them while they waved back from behind the glass of the car.

She bought a coffee and a magazine and waited for the boys' arrival. When the clock hands moved round to a time she considered as cutting things rather fine, she got up and went to the window again. The sky was very lowering, she hoped the car with the boys in it would arrive without mishap, and arrive soon. That black cloud had an ominous look about it. She knew with flying that such clouds can be detoured, but a car, when there was so little time left for checking in, could adopt no such detour.

The first large drops were falling just as the first summons for the southern departure began to be announced through the loudspeaker. At the same time Georgia recognized the expensive chauffeur-driven limousine pulling up. She peered out through the rain spatters and saw that this time a woman shared the back seat with the boys. When the limousine drew into the base of the steps she sat on until a porter with an umbrella came down to shelter her for the few yards to the canopy. She left the children to fend for themselves. Absurdly angry – it must be absurd to be angry over a six- and a seven-year-old surely able to look after themselves – Georgia hurried down to the lobby, and, seeing the boys enter behind the woman, she ran to them and started mopping them eagerly with her handkerchief.

'Georgie!' they greeted her, and it really was a greeting.

The woman turned, and Georgia recognized her as the woman in that leather-framed photograph that Grip Smith left so uncaringly around. Mrs. Agrippa Smith, though Grip never said so, never said 'my wife', only said 'the boys' mother'.

The boys also said mother. They said it now.

'This is our mother, Georgie,' they introduced.

'Georgia Paul,' acknowledged Georgia. She looked at the woman, still puzzled by a strange familiarity somewhere, not that of the likeness in her sons, but a feeling, for Georgia, that she had seen her before.

She was a very pretty woman; also, and this was much more arresting than her prettiness, exceptionally chic, outstandingly smart and richly groomed. She smiled at Georgia, a smile full of charm, but a turned-on smile. Georgia doubted if she really saw her.

'Sickening weather,' she said. 'Has your flight been called yet?'

'Yes, but it appears there's some delay.'

'Oh, heavens, I couldn't stand that, I loathe delays in airports.'

'It mightn't be for long.'

'I couldn't stand any length of time,' the boys' mother said. 'Bish, go and buy me some cigarettes, pet, you know what sort.'

'I'll go,' offered Georgia. She didn't want Bish sent for cigarettes. She didn't like a seven-year-old going up to a counter, possibly being questioned, possibly being—

'Thank you, dear, I've found some after all.' Delicate, beautifully-ringed fingers were deep in an expensive gold mesh bag.

There was another preparatory crackle on the loudspeaker, then an announcement in several languages. The plane, the English version said, was to be delayed a further period.

'Oh, no! I simply can't wait. But it won't matter, will it, you'll be here.'

Not giving Georgia any chance to protest, though she had no intention of protesting, the woman kissed both her sons' cheeks hurriedly, stuffed a note in each of their pockets, shook Georgia's hand, and left.

Only after she had gone, under the umbrella again, to the big waiting car, did Georgia realize that she had been given a banknote, too. She stood staring at it, at the size of it.

'Our mother,' explained Bish rather uninterestedly, 'is rich.'

He did not seem to mind her going. As for Seg, he did not even turn round. His eyes were on a poodle accompanying a girl seeing off a friend.

'Our plane is delayed,' Georgia told them. 'It won't be long, I think. What shall we do till then?'

'Pirates' Den,' they asked eagerly – Pirates' Den that they had scorned on their way up. They found a corner seat for the three of them beside a small coffee table, and there they sat for over an hour, Georgia getting nearly to Home on several occasions, each time throwing a number that took her to—

'Pirates' Den, Begin again,' they said in unison, and in glee. They didn't mind the delay because they were on their way back, even if they were only at the airport.

'Anyway,' said Bish, almost as though he had read Georgia's thoughts, 'we're not back *there*.' There, knew Georgia, was where they had been stopping. She threw an unfortunate number once more and was just being told:

'Pirates' Den Be—' when the summons came *really* to board this time. She put away the game, took the boys' hands and made for the boarding gate.

They had to run through rain to the air-bus, and going across the field they could see nothing but big grey drops.

They took off in rain, flew through rain, and then they were putting down in Nicosia, putting down from a sky as blue as cornflowers, on to a field already green-gold from a too generous winter sun.

When they came out of Customs, Grip Smith was waiting for them. He came forward and took so many bags from them that Georgia protested:

'You can't carry that much.'

'It's a pleasant chore, I've been so damned empty.'

'Empty?' she queried.

'The house or something.' He looked a little foolish. 'I never knew a man could feel so . . . well . . .'

'So Kate hasn't returned.' Georgia didn't mean anything particularly when she said that, but Grip Smith gave her a quick angry look.

'You would see it from that angle,' he said.

His old promptitude at picking her up brought her old colour flooding her cheeks.

'What other angle?' she inquired.

'It wouldn't occur to you that I was speaking as a man who had been lonely and was glad his household was returning again?'

'No, that wouldn't occur to me at all.'

Bish and Seg broke in anxiously for news of the Pink One, then, in lessening importance, news of Peaceful, Buttons, Purr, Olympia, Yiannis, Georgiou, Andreas.

'All well,' Grip reported. 'The Pink One particularly well. I'm not sure, but I feel when no one is about sometimes he has a trial run.'

The boys were overjoyed, so much so that Georgia felt she must give a note of warning.

'If once he flew, really flew, boys, he mightn't come back.'

'We know,' they said, 'but Zavallis at school said he couldn't ever do it, and we know he can.'

'But you wouldn't want to lose him just to show Zavallis.'

'You shouldn't call him Zavallis, Georgie, that's his second name, and it's only for boys. You should call him Mathos.'

'You wouldn't want the Pink One to fly just to spite Mathos?'

'We want it for himself, too,' they said solemnly, a little tremble there, but a lot of manliness. She felt proud of them.

There was not much traffic on the Limassol road, and the car ate up the miles.

'See the boys' mother?' Grip asked shortly.

'Briefly. There was a storm and we were delayed, so she didn't stop.'

'Then you surely saw the boys' mother,' said Grip.

He turned in at Amathus, and they climbed the hill Georgia did not realize until they had passed the safety ramp that she had not instinctively looked in. Grip pulled up the car, opened the door, helped them out, handed the bags to a waiting Yiannis.

Olympia was waiting, too, Georgiou, Andreas. They were all smiling and all expectant, and the moment the front door opened . . . for Olympia had had it drawn before . . . they found out why, and let out a shout of pleasure.

For there stood a tree – a belated tree, Grip explained.

'What's belated?' Seg asked him.

'An after tree. This is the tree you would have had, had you been here, your very own tree with your very own decorations. I've no doubt it's nothing like the tree you did have—'

'Hers had blinking lights and spotlights and—' Georgia noticed how Bish said 'hers' not 'ours'.

'There's all our presents under it,' called Seg. 'There's mine for Olympia, I remember packing it.'

'That's mine for Georgiou!'

Now they were leaping around the tree, calling attention to proud details of it, gloating over it, priding themselves for it, preferring every hand-tipped cone to the blinking lights, spotlights and floodlights of that other tree they had been given.

'And Miss Paul?' asked Grip Smith of Georgia. 'Does she find it enjoyable as well if humble?'

'It's a lovely tree,' said Georgia, not far from tears, 'and it's lovely of you. You're good father material after all.'

'Thank you,' said Grip, 'for I fully intend to be one, you know.'

He stood looking at Georgia, and, challenged, she looked back. But it was her own eyes that fanned down first.

CHAPTER ELEVEN

GRIP'S gesture to the boys was a complete success. Bish and Seg capered round the juniper that he had had Georgiou cut down and Andreas erect in a red tub with great excitement, calling to each other as they recognized some of their own handiwork.

'I did that cone' ... 'I made that reindeer' ... 'We stringed those silver bells, remember.'

They stood, tongues in cheeks, eyes dancing, as the staff opened their gifts. Afterwards, Bish said to Georgia: 'You could see that Olympia liked that shell I found and wrapped up for her much more than that old present my mother bought for me to give her.'

'Yes,' said Georgia rather faintly. The present had been a handsome wool stole in rich colours, and unmistakably rich in price. But Bish was happy in his present, in their tree.

'That one up there had just a lot of old lights, I like elated trees much better.'

That, thought Georgia, was a good description, so good she did not correct Bish.

It was another week before Kate returned to work, but it went pleasantly. Agrippa set aside his writing for that week and took them around the island. They went to Paphos to see the pelicans, to Polis to see Love's Spring, up to Panhandle to look across to Turkey.

Then they came home, because this present school vacation covered little more than the accepted public holidays. School started very early in Cyprus, or so Georgia considered, and she was a little concerned at the boys leaving home in the cold a.m. hours. However, they finished early for recompense, so caught the sun then. It was an arrangement that Agrippa approved, and it was pleasant, she had to admit, to have a long afternoon with the children after she had collected them and brought them home again.

While the snows were on they had several excursions to Troodos. The boys skied well, probably expertly trained on some exclusive slope, and laughed hilariously at Grip's and Georgia's less successful attempts. Georgia felt she could be forgiven – after all, a real Strine . . . she did not count Grip as one, not with all those years abroad . . . had to look for snow.

When she said this to him, he shrugged of himself: 'I was looking for something else.'

If he was waiting for her to ask what, he was to be disappointed. She turned and tried herself out again down the beginners' slope.

Kate returned, and once more the office was shut, and the sound of the typewriter and voices, low voices, came drifting out to prove the busyness that was being enacted there.

Justin came back.

January brought some rain, according to the country people not enough, but then rain, for farmers, was never enough, but February came in dry and almost warm. Yiannis declared that winter was over and spring upon them.

'That didn't take long,' said Georgia.

'Sometimes longer, sometimes *olihgo* . . . little. But by Clean Monday we are looking summer almost in her face.'

Clean Monday was the beginning of Lent, and on that day everyone went to the fields for a picnic, but a picnic of only bread, olives and vegetables. The house on the Amathus hill decided to join in the custom, too, and Justin drove up to participate with them, and under the big carob tree all the staff, and those served by them, and Justin, sat happily together in a warm sun.

The Pink One had been let out and was roving around

scratching at the rich brown earth.

'Do flamingoes have Lent?' asked Seg.

'I don't know,' said Grip carefully, and Georgia soon learned why he spoke like that. For it had been all very well for the boys to boast that they wanted the Pink One to fly, even fly away, but what if it came to actuality? 'We can find out,' he went on, still careful. 'The squadron has flown in. The Akrotiri lake is filled with this year's flight.'

There was a silence, and Georgia knew sharply the beginnings of pain the children were experiencing.

'Perhaps we'd better go out there,' gulped Bish, 'take the Pink One with us, let him see his relations.'

'No, not that yet, the flamingoes will be here quite a while, and I think we should look them over ourselves first, judge their size.'

'Yes,' agreed the boys eagerly, anxious to postpone that other.

After the meal they divided into two cars and drove down to the salt pan, quite a little lake now following the winter wet.

There they stood enchanted. In summer, from the salt, the pan shimmered silver, but now it shimmered rose pink. The vast flocks of wading birds rested together like a roseate island on it, but when one, either alarmed, or merely stretching his wings, reached up and flew, the others followed to weave a pink necklace against the blue sky.

'I think,' gulped Bish, 'the Pink One would like that.'

'I think so,' agreed Grip. He gave the boy his binoculars. 'I think he's as big and strong, too, as they are. What do you say?'

'I say,' said Bish bravely ... but a tear rolled past his nose.

Because it would be some time before the exodus to the Rift Valley in Kenya began, Grip suggested they leave the Pink One where he was till then.

'Yes,' they agreed eagerly again.

Every day during February the snow tablecloths became smaller and more meagre. Winter was flying away. It was never long, Olympia told Georgia, but this year it had come, and then *po, po, po* ... Cypriot for pouf! ... it had gone again. There had not even been the usual rain, and the farmers were unhappy over that.

Georgia was happy over the spring, though, for never before had she seen so much spring. The valleys, the slopes, the fields, fairly burst over with flowers. You could not walk a meadow without trampling down wild anemones, iris, red poppies and asphodel. Cyclamen pushed up in mauve and violet clumps.

Only Mount Olympus wore a snow coronet now, and a small one, so the winter was surely over, and the forests soon should be full of pale green leaf.

'Something Strines don't get,' reminded Grip of the eucalyptus country, 'we only receive change of tree trunks. In which case I think another picnic is called for.'

'Shall we all go like we did before?' said Seg.

The staff declined, Clean Monday was enough picnic for them for the year, but Kate and Justin joined in, and, at the last moment, Zavallis.

'Did you ask Zavallis?' Georgia asked the boys.

'You should call him Mathos, only boys call boys by their surnames. I told you before.' They both looked severe.

'Did you invite Mathos?' she corrected herself.

'No, we didn't. He's come himself because of the lion. He doesn't believe the Pink One can fly, so we don't believe in the lion.'

'And?' asked Georgia.

'And it's to be proved,' said Seg.

'Each side proved?'

'Yes, but the lion proved first because we tossed up a mil and Zavallis lost.'

'So he's to show you the lion in the forest?'

The boys nodded.

'Perhaps it's a mouflon, a wild sheep.' Georgia hoped so, she wanted very much to see one of these ancient animals, still now in existence in the Cypriot forests.

'No, it's a lion, Zavallis said. Once he saw it with blood dripping down.'

'Yes, you told me before. Now tell Yiannis to pack lunch for one more.' Or, thought Georgia fastidiously, Zavallis can eat my share. She did not fancy blood dripping down.

They left early for the forest, and it was a beautiful drive, but dry for this time of year. Spring should be more moist, Georgia thought, more dewy: although there was an abundance of green there was quite a lot of dead or parched brown as well.

'Camelot,' drawled Grip from behind the wheel, 'didn't police its weather properly this year – some of that timber is almost tinder-dry.'

Mathos proved an alert little boy with sharp black eyes and a sense of adventure. Three times he had to be told not to explore past a certain prescribed distance.

He spoke back to Bish, not being fluent yet with his English, and Bish reported that Zavallis doubted if the lion would come out from where he was, and if they couldn't go, they wouldn't see him.

'Making Zavallis the winner,' said Grip, 'by us not allowing our kids to prove him wrong by not finding any lion.'

Our kids. No one took any notice of it ... but Georgia did. They all laughed, and, replete from the fine meal that Yiannis had provided, lay back in the sun and drifted into casual talk, and eventually sleep.

The children played in the creek, from which the snow waste had drained now, leaving only a tiny musical trickle. Knowing how boys love brooks, love to launch bark boats, how they will play safely for hours, Georgia relaxed with the rest, talked occasionally, drifted off as well.

What happened then happened so fast, and so frighteningly, that afterwards it was hard to piece it all together.

The boys disobeyed by going farther than they had been told – that was not to be argued, as they both, Bish and Seg, painfully discovered – but it was not the disobedience that almost caused the tragedy, it was what they did. Perhaps it would have been fairer to say Zavallis did, but nonetheless Seg and Bish were soundly whacked.

The first Georgia knew was Grip jumping to this feet and crying 'Good grief!' Then she heard crackling. She saw smoke and flame.

Brushwood was burning, the same tindery brush that Grip had commented on. Even as she leapt up to watch by Grip's side the flaming brushwood caught a dried-out, half-dead tree and a tongue of red leapt eagerly up the lower boughs. Sparks showed.

Thirst-dry branches on other trees seemed fairly to reach out to gather a flame for themselves. Smoke began to cover everything in a thick blue pall.

In no time a dozen trees were ablaze, some of the crackling was thunder-sharp. Bits of burning bark drifted in the wind, igniting old thistle, thick beds of dried pine needles, seared scilla. A red-hot heat was beginning to fan towards them.

Georgia started to run forward, calling the boys, but Grip caught her roughly and pushed her back.

'I'll get them,' he said grimly. 'You'll only make matters worse – stay where you are. You take over, Justin.'

He disappeared into the trees.

Justin said, 'He's right, we can't help in there . . . here, either, for that matter. We'll get out. At least we can raise an alarm, enlist help. Don't stop to carry anything. Just run.'

They all ran . . . at least they thought they all ran, that the *three* of them ran. But when they got to an untouched clearing, Kate was not with them. She had stumbled, they were to learn later, but in the eddies of smoke they did not see her, and in the loud noise now of falling branches they did not hear her cry out.

There was a stream in the clearing, and they jumped thankfully into it, then Justin said: 'Kate!'

That was all he did say, he did not wait to wonder what had happened, where she was, he did not even stop to tell Georgia to remain where she was, he simply ran back into the smoke, into the ashy, crackle-loud, licking flames, and though it was only several minutes before he came out again, with Kate in his arms, to Georgia it seemed a lifetime, a lifetime of torment, a torment because of Grip and the boys, too, but she didn't know about them, and she did about Justin and Kate, she knew they were in that inferno.

But they were out now, and she was kneeling with Justin beside Kate, Kate with her hair and skin badly scorched, moaning a little, tears weeping from her closed violet eyes.

'My God, Gigi, she's bad,' he muttered.

'I don't think so. I mean it's bad enough, but – but I don't think so.' Georgia saw that Justin himself had no eyebrows.

Birds were flying above them, shrieking a warning, telling everyone there was something bad here. At least, that was what it seemed to Georgia.

And it must have seemed so, too, for the rest of the forest. In quite a short time, though not alerted, help was arriving, small village brigades, trucks with water, men with wet bags. The screeching birds and a finger of rising smoke had spread the news.

An ambulance arrived. It took Kate and Justin. Georgia refused to go.

The fire had not extended far – though, said Grip later, and very grimly, no thanks to those who had started it. Zavallis had started it, Grip knew that, but Bish and Seg had stood by, so they were as bad as Zavallis.

He said this slowly, deliberately, judiciously, he told them that starting a fire . . . it had been to smoke out a lion

. . . was something that an Australian must never do, a Cypriot, either, but he would let Zavallis's father drive home that point. A look on Zavallis's face indicated that his father certainly would, when he arrived home. But Grip did not wait for home for their two, he chose a good stick, and thereupon whacked both boys long and hard.

It was a thorough punishment, and Georgia watched a little aghast. Not aghast because of the punishment, it was deserved, and it had to be given, but aghast at how this unwhacked, undoubtedly never spanked pair would react.

The reaction astounded her. Punishment over, they stood looking amazed at Grip, amazed . . . and something else.

'Orfanides at school often gets a whack from his dad,' said Seg.

'No one has even done that to us,' said Bish.

'They have now,' Grip nodded. 'I have.'

'Yes, you have.'

They still looked at him in surprise. Then they went off to lick their wounds . . . but rather pridefully so. Georgia could hear them saying at school: 'We were whacked. Our father whacked us.' – Except, she recalled, they never said father, in fact they didn't address Grip as anything at all.

'My God, those kids have a lesson coming to them,' Grip swore after them.

'You gave it,' she said ruefully.

'I'd do it again, and right now – an Australian playing with fire!'

'It was Mathos, really, he has a vivid imagination.'

'After what I'm going to report to his father, young Mathos is going to be vivid elsewhere,' he snapped. 'Well, I expect it could be worse. It could be more than just Kate affected. How is she, do you think?'

'Her hair caught it, her skin is scorched, apart from that she seemed all right, but there's always shock.'

'Yes,' he agreed soberly, 'shock.' He was silent a moment, then he called shortly: 'All right, you kids, get in the car, we're going home.'

'I don't want to,' wailed Mathos.

'I wouldn't, either, in your shoes,' said Grip grimly.

Georgia heard Seg say to Mathos: 'How hard does your father whack, Zavallis? He' ... he nodded his head ... 'came down pretty bang-on on us.'

They left the boys to the administrations of Olympia ... not too kindly administrations, Grip sternly ordered the soft Cypriot woman ... then left the apprehensive Mathos at the cottage at the bottom of the hill.

They drove to Limassol hospital, where they found Justin, white-faced, drained, a different man from the man of a few hours ago.

'It's not as simple as I thought it was,' Justin said, distressed.

'Shock?'

'Also lungs filled with ash ... also her hands ...' Justin clenched his own hands, then winced. They were raw themselves.

'We'll wait with you, old man,' said Grip.

'No ... no, I want to be by myself,' Justin said dully, and looked at them apologetically, willing them to understand.

'We understand,' said Grip.

'You can't really.' Justin gulped painfully. 'But I'm still hoping you'll try. Perhaps if Gigi could just wait a while ...'

'I'll be in the car,' said Grip, and he left them together.

For a long time Justin did not speak, then he turned to Georgia, nervously moistening his lips. 'If anything happens—'

'It won't.'

'If Katherine—'

'Nothing is going to happen. Kate will be all right. She'll lose some of that lovely hair, but it will grow again. Her face, too, is burned, but it will heal. The lungs will clear, the shock diminish. *Justin, she'll be all right.*'

Justin said simply: 'I love her, you know.'

'Yes, I know.'

'Do you really, though, Gigi, or are you being kind?'

'It's you who have been kind – too kind. You never did love me, Justin, but you were too nice to say.'

'Not exactly, Gigi, I was very crushed on you, who wouldn't be on a lovely eighteen-year-old who—'

'Who threw herself at you?'

'You didn't, honey, you were just attracted by an older man, and the older man was flattered, terribly flattered, even to the extent of being a fair way in love himself. I mean it does happen, Gigi, when a man is away from his heart, it does happen.'

'And what did happen afterwards, Justin?'

'I went back, and Katherine, right out of the blue, refused to marry me.'

'Why?'

'She didn't say – she didn't have to, I knew. Knew she could sense that I wasn't quite the same as I had been when I left her. The thing was she didn't know how deep it had gone, and in the fool way lovers arrange their lives, she wouldn't ask, so I wouldn't tell.

'I was terribly hurt when she said it was over, so hurt I wouldn't fight for her, try to tell her the facts, the facts of a lovely island, a lovely girl, a lovely summer, but that was all.'

Reminder of summer, Georgia thought.

'We simply parted. I took up my next rep assignment in Athens, other places after that. From the time I left Katherine that day I didn't see her again until I saw her this go. It rocked me, Gigi. When I first returned here, I got to remembering *our* summer together, your summer and mine, building it up to something it really never was . . . for it wasn't, you know.'

'I know. I know it, anyway, now.'

179

'I think I fell in love with you *really* then. Fell in love – but never loved. There's a difference.'

Again Georgia murmured, 'I know.'

'I wanted to go on from that moment, and I would have, only—'

'Only you saw Kate.'

'I saw Katherine, and I knew it was only Katherine for me. Oh, Gigi, I'm sorry, I've certainly messed up your life.'

'No,' she smiled, 'you only supplied a first greening to a very young girl. Spring never lasts long, so you didn't either, Justin. The woman I am now can hardly remember to then.'

'Yet you were as glad to see me as I was you,' he told her.

'Reminder of summer.' She said it aloud this time. 'Yes, I was glad,' she admitted, 'but you must have seen that I wasn't . . . that I didn't . . .'

'Yes, I saw.'

There seemed one thing, however, he had not seen, and Georgia suppressed a little shiver. After all the heat of the day it seemed absurd, but she could not help feeling cold, cold because of a memory. A memory of a man in a mask looking at a girl also in a mask, and whispering: 'Dear, dear Kate.'

Surely Justin must sense that Grip felt the same as he did.

Then what about Kate? Which one did Kate hold to her heart?

Georgia was not to know then, nor for days after, for Kate was detained for some time. Then finally she emerged from the forest nightmare, emerged with a rather trembling smile, a flattering short haircut, dressings on her face and hands. *And arms outstretched to Justin.*

So it was Justin. Poor Grip, Georgia thought.

She broke it to Grip on the night following the afternoon

that Kate told it all to her.

Kate had said: 'When Justin came home that time, I had the feeling he wasn't mine any more. I was younger then, you know how possessive youth is. After he went, after he walked out following my refusal, I grew wiser, but then I had this wretched pride. If I hadn't met Justin this time, it could have gone on and on.'

'Or you could have married Agrippa Smith,' said Georgia.

'Grip?' Kate looked at her in amazement. 'Oh, you funny thing, fancy *you* saying that!'

'All those hours in the office,' protested Georgia.

'Typing current affairs.'

'And a book.'

'Yes,' said Kate, dreamily now, 'a very beautiful book. A very simple book, actually. A love story.'

'I read some of it.'

'I know – Grip told me once. He told me you had it on your lap reading it, something a good copy-typist doesn't do. But you sat and read and read, read with all of you as well as just your eyes.' She smiled at Georgia.

'He was angry? Grip was?'

'No, he was—' Kate looked at Georgia. 'Have you seen the book?' she asked.

'Seen it?'

'It's published. The author's copies have arrived.'

'They can't have, not that quickly.'

'He's an important writer, remember, important writers have pride of place on publishers' lists – beside, with a book like—'

'Kate told me your book is called *Pink Bird, Go South*,' Georgia said to Grip that night.

'True,' he nodded sparsely.

'She loved it.'

'I think so.' Still sparsely.

181

'But' . . . well, he had to know some time, and the only way, the only decent way, to tell a direct man like Agrippa Smith was to *tell* him . . . 'Kate herself loves Justin.'

'I know,' he said calmly, 'I always knew.'

She looked at him angrily, angry at his easy dismissal of something that must have meant a lot to him, but, because his pride came first, he found he could successfully put aside.

'You didn't know,' she said accusingly, 'I know you didn't know, because, you see, you made a mistake that night.' She wondered why she was persisting like this.

'What night?' he asked.

'The masquerade – the *Karnivali*.'

'What mistake did I make?'

'You thought I was Kate. You said, "Dear, dear Kate." I was amused at the time because I thought you were Justin.'

'Amused?' He came in sharply with that.

'Yes, I was amused.' She looked frankly back at him. 'But you . . . well, you were—'

'Yes,' he agreed.

'And you said that,' she persisted again. 'I heard you.'

'I said it, and I meant it, because she was dear, dear Kate to me – she had just told me something that I wanted to hear more than anything else in the world.' He stared expectantly at her, expecting her question, Georgia looked back at him . . . but she did not ask.

Anyway, she thought drearily, how could anyone ask questions of – that sort to a married man, an estranged marriage perhaps, a separate marriage, an ex-marriage, but still somewhere in it – marriage. There were no questions that could be asked.

The next morning when Georgia was driving the boys to school, they called out suddenly and urgently for her to stop, then they pointed tremblingly to the sky. Georgia braked and looked up with them.

There, wheeling and weaving in an incredibly beautiful pattern, the pink birds were unrolling a satin ribbon across the wide vast blue.

'They're getting ready to go,' Bish said with a tremor.

Seg said nothing, the tears were rolling down his cheeks.

Georgia turned the car in silence and went back up the hill. There would be no school today, she knew.

She called out to Grip, and he emerged at once from the office, and only that she was strained herself, she would have seen the strain on his face, seen a letter in his hand.

'The flamingoes are leaving,' she said.

The four of them went down to the coop and let the Pink One out.

'Can we take him to Akrotiri to give him his chance?' Georgia whispered to Grip.

'Just let things happen,' Grip said, and he sat down on the coop edge.

The Pink One went foraging. He did not look up at the rosy cloud that passed over, that crossed into the distance, then in several minutes passed over again. The birds were preparing to set a course into wind.

It was all very emotionally upsetting, Georgia found it so, so she knew how the boys must feel. And did feel.

Suddenly and fiercely, Bish called accusingly, 'Do something!' at Grip.

Grip turned angrily and called back, 'Watch your tongue, and address me properly, please.'

The boys were crying openly now, they were following the flamingo to a new scratching patch halfway down the slope. Over his shoulder a shamed Bish called, 'I'm sorry, Uncle Grip.'

As if from a long way off Georgia heard it, then heard it in echo again.

I'm sorry, Uncle Grip.

Uncle Grip. *Uncle* Grip. She sat down on the coop edge, too.

Grip Smith was looking at her, reading her, reading the way she had thought all along.

'Oh, good heavens,' he said.

'I thought she was ... I thought the boys' mother was ...'

'She was ... is ... my twin.' – So that was why she had found a familiarity apart from Bish and Seg.

'Sigrid was the most spoiled brat a family ever raised,' he said wearily. 'We were a strictly male bunch before Sig, strings of boys for centuries or so. When Sigrid arrived an hour after I did, heaven opened. The Smiths had a girl!

'She was adulated. She was absolutely bowed to. To some it would make no difference, or only a little difference, or a forgivable difference, but not Sigrid. Every family has a mistake, and Sigrid was the Smith mistake.' He looked around to see if the boys were still out of earshot.

'You're very bitter over her,' Georgia said.

'She married my best friend. Paul was not just my best friend, he was – well, best.' There was pain on Grip's face.

'He is the boys' father?'

'Was. He died – died of heartache. You can laugh if you like, but it's true.'

'I'm not laughing,' said Georgia.

'He was a pilot, a test pilot. The letter came.' For a moment he looked down at the letter he held. 'Soon afterwards he went up and ...' He spread his hands.

'She, Sigrid, married soon after. And soon after that again. This is now Number Three marriage, but I feel it will stop at three. Because on this occasion there's more than just a lot of money, there's a nice position in a jetsetters' set-up, all the fascinating sidekicks.'

'And the boys?

'That's dealt with in another letter. Oh, my sister is a dab

184

hand at letters.' He crushed the one he held.

'What does it say?' she asked.

'She doesn't want them. She doesn't want the kids.'

'But you were taking them to Australia.'

'For a period only. Now—'

'Why doesn't she want them?'

'No specific reason, nothing direct, Sigrid is too clever to be direct.

'She uses her doctor . . . he says she must rest. Her psychiatrist . . . he says she's emotionally drained . . . Her neurologist, her masseur, her – her husband.' A short bitter laugh.

' "Anyway, Grip dear" . . . he made his voice insincere . . ' "you always wanted them brought up Australians. I, of course, will defray the cost." '

'Then,' broke in Georgia spontaneously, 'why not?'

'Why not?' He looked scornfully at her. 'Because I'm a man. I can't bring up two youngsters.'

A minute went by in absolute silence, then Georgia said: 'I can.'

She stopped short in amazement at herself. She looked at him. He looked narrowly back.

'You can't have them,' he told her carefully. 'I want them to lead a normal life. Male and female parents.'

'I understand that.' Again she stopped in surprise at herself. But she also stopped to wait for him to say something. Didn't he, couldn't he see she was waiting?

He put his hand in his pocket and withdrew a book, only a small volume – a slim one. He gave it to her.

'*Pink Bird Go South*,' she read. She opened it, then looked up at him. 'For Georgia,' it was inscribed.

'For me?'

'You're the only one I know with that name.' His voice was gruff.

'But why? *Why?*'

'Because,' he said barely, 'you're the only one.'

'But you said to Kate—'

'I said dear, dear Kate, thank you for ever for telling me from a woman that that other woman feels as I do.'

'You didn't say that,' she recalled.

'I said it in my mind.'

'Kate hadn't said that to you about me.'

'Oh, yes, she had.'

'But she couldn't have known how I felt—'

'She knew.' – He stopped short. 'What is this?' he asked almost violently. 'You're admitting it's the truth?'

'No. Yes. No. I mean . . .'

'*Uncle Grip!*' Bish's voice came sharply, agonizingly, and yet somewhere in the agony a triumph and a gladness. 'Uncle Grip, Georgie!' he called again.

They both stood up.

The pink contingent was returning. In the strange way that birds know such things, they must have known that the one they had left behind last time was ready to go now. They knew where to find him.

Over the hill house they swooped in a rosy ribbon, and hesitating only a moment, flexing and unflexing only a moment, the Pink One rose, too. Rose up, and joined them. Joined the pink necklace.

'I can't tell which is him,' sobbed Seg, but there was pride in his wet face.

'Wait till I tell that Zavallis,' said Bish . . . and started to sob.

Yet there was something manly in their grief, something deeply satisfied. And accepted.

'We're going that way, too, aren't we, Uncle Grip? Going south.'

'Yes.'

'And Georgie?'

Grip looked at Georgia, asked, 'You, too, Pink Bird?' in a voice only she could hear, and she looked back and nodded.

Grip answered: 'And Georgie.'

'All four of us.'

'All four.' Grip had his own Pink One's hand now in his.

Then a wonderful thing happened. Though the necklace had done its last weaving, or so, from the distance this time, they had thought, the squadron flew back again, and out of it swooped one bird.

The wader circled them once only, just once, then rejoined his flight. They saw the contingent merging into the distance again one flier a little separate, or so it seemed.

Soon it would become part of them, entirely part, and that was what they wanted, but for a few pink moments it was their dear one, their wading bird.

Their flamingo flying south.

Why the smile?

... because she has just received her **Free Harlequin Romance Catalogue!**

... and now she has a complete listing of the many, many Harlequin Romances still available.

... and now she can pick out titles by her favorite authors or fill in missing numbers for her library.

You too may have a **Free Harlequin Romance Catalogue** (and a smile!), simply by writing to:

HARLEQUIN READER SERVICE

DEPARTMENT C
M.P.O. BOX 707
NIAGARA FALLS N.Y.
14302

Canadian Address:
STRATFORD, ONTARIO
CANADA

Be sure to include your name and address!

Please Note: Harlequin Romance Catalogue of available titles is revised every three months.

BY POPULAR DEMAND
4 *Harlequin Presents...*
EVERY MONTH

OVER THE YEARS many favourite Harlequin Romance authors have written novels which have not been available to Harlequin Romance. Now, because of the overwhelming response to Harlequin Presents, they are allowing us to publish these original works in the Harlequin Presents series. Authors such as Roberta Leigh, Rachel Lindsay, Rosalind Brett and Margaret Rome will be joining Anne Hampson, Anne Mather and Violet Winspear enabling us to publish 4 titles per month on a continuing basis.

Look for these books at your local bookseller, or use the handy order coupon. See title listing on following page.

PLEASE NOTE: All Harlequin Presents novels from #83 onwards are 95c. Books below that number, **where available** are priced at 75c through Harlequin Reader Service until December 31st, 1975.

To: HARLEQUIN READER SERVICE, Dept. N 504
   M.P.O. Box 707, Niagara Falls, N.Y. 14302
   Canadian address: Stratford, Ont., Canada

☐ Please send me the free Harlequin Romance Presents Catalogue.

☐ Please send me the titles checked on following page.
I enclose $ .... (No C.O.D.'s). All books listed are 75c each. To help defray postage and handling cost, please add 25c.

Name ....

Address ....

City/Town ....

State/Prov. .... Zip ....

Harlequin Presents..

Some of the world's greatest romance authors.

ALL BOOKS LISTED 75c

These titles are available at your local bookseller, or through
the Harlequin Reader Service, M.P.O. Box 707, Niagara Falls,
N.Y. 14302; Canadian address 649 Ontario St., Stratford, Ont.

E

Have You Missed Any of These
Harlequin Romances?

Have You Missed Any of These
Harlequin Romances?

- [ ] 1211 BRIDE OF KYLSAIG
  Iris Danbury
- [ ] 1214 THE MARSHALL FAMILY
  Mary Burchell
- [ ] 1216 ORANGES AND LEMONS
  Isobel Chace
- [ ] 1218 BEGGARS MAY SING
  Sara Seale
- [ ] 1222 DARK CONFESSOR
  Elinor Davis
- [ ] 1236 JEMIMA
  Leonora Starr
- [ ] 1244 WHEN LOVE IS BLIND
  Mary Burchell
- [ ] 1246 THE CONSTANT HEART
  Eleanor Farnes
- [ ] 1248 WHERE LOVE IS
  Norrey Ford
- [ ] 1253 DREAM COME TRUE
  Patricia Fenwick
- [ ] 1254 THE MASTER OF KEILLS
  Jean S. Macleod
- [ ] 1260 WE LIVE IN SECRET
  Dorothy Rivers
- [ ] 1276 STEEPLE RIDGE
  Jill Tahourdin
- [ ] 1277 STRANGER'S TRESPASS
  Jane Arbor
- [ ] 1278 THE KING OF THE CASTLE
  Anita Charles
- [ ] 1282 THE SHINING STAR
  Hilary Wilde
- [ ] 1284 ONLY MY HEART TO GIVE
  Nan Asquith
- [ ] 1285 OUT OF A DREAM
  Jean Curtis
- [ ] 1288 THE LAST OF THE KINTYRES
  Catherine Airlie
- [ ] 1293 I KNOW MY LOVE
  Sara Seale
- [ ] 1301 HOTEL BY THE LOCH
  Iris Danbury
- [ ] 1304 SHARLIE FOR SHORT
  Dorothy Rivers
- [ ] 1309 THE HILLS OF MAKETU
  Gloria Bevan
- [ ] 1312 PEPPERCORN HARVEST
  Ivy Ferrari
- [ ] 1322 WIND THROUGH THE
  VINEYARDS
  Juliet Armstrong
- [ ] 1601 THE NEWCOMER
  Hilda Pressley
- [ ] 1606 THE QUIET VELD, Jean Dunbar
- [ ] 1607 NOT LESS THAN ALL
  Margaret Malcolm
- [ ] 1623 FLOWERS FOR THE FESTIVAL
  Belinda Dell
- [ ] 1633 RED GINGER BLOSSOM
  Joyce Dingwell
- [ ] 1652 A PEARL FOR LOVE
  Mary Cummins
- [ ] 1704 EXCEPT MY LOVE
  Mary Burchell
- [ ] 1718 LORD OF THE FOREST
  Hilda Nickson
- [ ] 1722 FOLLOW A STRANGER
  Charlotte Lamb
- [ ] 1724 WEDDING AT BLUE RIVER
  Dorothy Quentin
- [ ] 1725 THE EXTRAORDINARY EN-
  GAGEMENT   Marjorie Lewty
- [ ] 1726 MAN IN CHARGE, Lilian Feake
- [ ] 1727 STRANGE BEWILDERMENT
  Katrina Britt
- [ ] 1729 THE YOUNG DOCTOR
  Sheila Douglas
- [ ] 1730 FLAME IN FIJI, Gloria Bevan
- [ ] 1731 THE FORBIDDEN VALLEY
  Essie Summers
- [ ] 1732 BEYOND THE SUNSET
  Flora Kidd
- [ ] 1733 CALL AND I'LL COME
  Mary Burchell
- [ ] 1734 THE GIRL FROM ROME
  Nan Asquith
- [ ] 1735 TEMPTATIONS OF THE MOON
  Hilary Wilde
- [ ] 1736 THE ENCHANTED RING
  Lucy Gillen
- [ ] 1737 WINTER OF CHANGE
  Betty Neels
- [ ] 1738 THE MUTUAL LOOK
  Joyce Dingwell

ZZ